THE ANNALS OF SKORNE

Records of the Three Realms

Standalone Novella

THE ANNALS OF SKORNE

Records of the Three Realms

Standalone Novella

Joshua Killingsworth

MYSTIC FOX PUBLISHING

ISBN: 978-1-7341255-4-2 (Paperback)

ISBN: 978-1-7341255-5-9 (eBook)

JoshuaKillingsworth.com @WriterJMK

Mystic Fox Publishing

To Balian and Avexis

PART I
Memories of the Lost

CHAPTER ONE

THE CARRIAGE STOPPED IN front of a great wooden manor tucked in next to the frosty woods. The manor seemed too large compared to the small village at the bottom of the hill. Like the surrounding land, snow and ice covered the manor. Crescentwood sat on the edge of the frozen desert, which was the northernmost settlement in the province of Kyradon. Baldric rubbed his eyes. He was here. Finally, after two months of travel, he was home.

"This is it," the driver said, opening the door. He held out his hand for Baldric to take.

Baldric ignored the driver's assistance and stood from the carriage on his own. He stretched his arms above his head and arched his back. His legs had grown stiff from riding for so long. The scent of the nearby pine forest filled his nostrils.

A tall, balding man dressed in fine clothes and thick furs approached him from the manor. He stopped just shy of Baldric and bowed in reverence.

"Prince Baldric, welcome to Crescentwood Manor," the man said.

"I'm not a prince," Baldric replied, walking past the man. "Not anymore."

"Of course, my lord." The man raised himself upright and hurried after Baldric. "I am the steward of the manor. You may call me Irfan —"

"I'm aware of who you are," Baldric interrupted. He shivered in the freezing, dry air. It would take some time to get used to the extreme cold. The south was very different. While the nights were frigid, the days were hot—still dry, though. He supposed they had that in common. "Please, it has been a long journey. Can you show me to my room?"

"The whole manor is yours," Irfan said. "You own all the land of the town as well. And your father is king of the realm. You may go wherever you please."

Baldric rolled his eyes and nodded. "Yes, yes. But where do I sleep?"

"You may choose any room you like. If it is occupied, we shall move the occupant."

"Gods, you're useless," Baldric mumbled. He shook his head. "Sorry. This is a manor, yes? Surely it has a room that is not currently occupied."

"Of course." Irfan smiled.

"Any of those will do. Lead the way," Baldric motioned toward the manor's double doors.

Etched into the wood was the crescent moon of Adgul. Adgul had little in the way of oceans, and the colossal land masses that comprised the world consisted mostly of vast deserts with sparse settlements scattered throughout. Vegetation was limited to areas around rivers and other small waterways that snaked their way through the continents. To the far north and south were the frozen wastes—like Crescentwood—that existed on the edges of the arctic deserts. Baldric's father was king and Sage of Adgul; loyal to the Guardian of the Three Realms. Baldric scoffed at the notion. The king's *sagacious* wisdom was derived from loyalty. How did that prove wisdom?

Irfan nodded and turned on his heels toward the manor, opening the double doors. The entrance was grand, with a red sofa and roaring fireplace greeting them. Fur rugs lined the wooden floor, while matching banners dotted the walls.

Baldric grabbed his worn leather bags and followed behind the steward.

"My lord," the driver called out, running after them. "Please allow me to carry your things."

"I've got them," Baldric said, recoiling from the driver's hand.

"That's hardly fitting for someone of your standing, sir," Irfan said, agreeing with the driver. "I will have a servant see to them at once."

"I'm not an invalid," Baldric argued, slinging a bag over his shoulder. His brow furrowed as a scowl formed on his face. "I can carry my own things."

Irfan stood silent, mouth agape, but did not protest. He nodded and led Baldric to a large room on the upper floor. Like the entrance, more fur rugs warmed the floor. A bed sat in the center of the room flanked by a stone stove while two large armoires were placed on adjacent walls. Baldric stepped inside and tossed his bags to the floor.

"Would you like a tour of the manor?" Irfan asked.

"Maybe later." Baldric knelt down and undid his boots, tossing them next to the door. "I just want some rest for now."

"Of course. I shall leave you to it." Irfan turned and shut the door on his way out, leaving Baldric alone with his thoughts.

He slung his wool cloak over the foot of the bed and slumped down onto the covers. He rubbed his hand through his dark hair. Baldric couldn't get away from his station, no matter how hard he tried. No one would ever see him as anything other than a prince. That life wasn't for him. He slammed his head against the pillow, and it sunk into the soft feathery cushion. He would start a new life here. Whether or not he wanted to. Either way, it would never be *his* life. Only one dictated to him by his father.

All he ever had was the illusion of choice. He spent years studying in the best universities in the realm, only then to be sent off to the best the other realms had to offer. His whole life was spent in preparation for him to assume the throne and rule Adgul. It was a life dictated to him. He was told what to do, what to learn—what he should care about. Waiting at the end of his endeavors was nothing more than a hollow throne where he would serve as a puppet king to the Immortal Warrior—the Guardian of the Three Realms.

Baldric grimaced, just thinking of him.

Living up to his namesake, the Immortal Warrior had reigned for over a thousand years, having united the Three Realms under his law. The lesser rulers—the kings and emperors—only maintained their power through their subserviency and preserving the status quo.

If his studies taught him anything, the best leaders did more than bow to tradition. They never stopped trying to improve the lives of their followers. The Immortal Warrior established peace and tranquility, then spent an entire age ensuring nothing else changed and threaten undoing that stability. But a new age was desperately needed.

Adgul was a harsh and arid environment. No matter where they lived in Adgul, people struggled just to survive. Famine and water shortages were common.

With the Immortal Warrior as Guardian, nothing would ever change for Adgul. Even time and age were submissive to him. There was no hope for his people. The Immortal Warrior would rule forever.

Besides, it was easy enough to identify the problems, but it was another matter entirely to offer solutions, and Baldric had none. The second lesson his studies taught him was his own limitations. He was far too incompetent a leader to serve as king. It was a role he was ill suited for. So, he made the only decision he could—the only choice offered in his life. He refused the throne.

He pushed the thoughts out of his mind as he stared up at the wooden beams crossing the ceiling. His eyes became heavy, and he was soon fast asleep.

Shouting voices downstairs awoke him. They were yelling back and forth, but were too distant to determine what they were saying. Baldric sighed. It seemed rest would have to wait.

He hurried down the stairs to find Irfan arguing with two other men. One was garbed in green and gold robes—traditional religious attire. The other was a soldier. He wore brown lamellar armor and had an arming sword strapped to his side.

"I told you!" yelled Irfan, his expression livid. "I will not allow you to harass that poor girl!"

"She is no more a girl than you are a saint!" the priest retorted.

Baldric interfered, stepping between them.

"What is this commotion about?" he demanded. His eyes met the priest's, who glared back. "The three of you could wake the dead."

"Who the devil are you?" the man in the armor asked.

Irfan puffed out his chest.

"This is Lord Baldric," he responded, seeming pleased for the backup, though Baldric had yet to decide which party to agree with—if either.

"This is the banished prince?" The armored man looked Baldric up and down, as if to size him up.

Baldric grimaced. "Not a prince."

"This is Zuan. He is your bailiff." Irfan gestured first to the soldier, then nodded toward the robed man. "And this is

Father Piet. We were just discussing how best to deal with a situation."

"What sort of situation?" Baldric asked, raising an eyebrow.

"A troublesome young woman." Zuan held up a piece of parchment with tallies and numbers scribbled on it. "She hasn't paid rent in six months."

"How much is her rent?" Baldric asked, taking the parchment from him. He scanned the sheet. It provided a summary of her family's payments dating back for three years. Baldric noted her name at the top of the page—Seraphina Larsen. The names of her father and mother had been scratched out and a death date written next to each name.

"A fourth in kind," Zuan replied, pointing to where it was written as such on the parchment. "But that's the problem. She doesn't produce anything. Ever since her parents died, she has refused to labor. She claims to be a scholar like her father, but even he would work the fields to provide rent."

Baldric frowned as he listened to Zuan's words.

"If she doesn't work. How does she eat or light her house? Who produces the goods she uses?" Baldric stared at the numbers on the parchment, but they were meaningless to him.

"The manor collects a portion of all goods produced by the tenants of the land," Irfan explained. "What is stored is divided amongst the villagers for communal use. The remainder is either stockpiled or bartered. I don't remember the last time this has occurred, but we could remove her from these lands."

"And condemn her to die of exposure?" Baldric glowered. Irfan stammered, but didn't say a word.

The three men stared at the ground and remained silent.

"Am I missing something?" Baldric asked, shifting his weight to his back foot.

"She's a witch," Piet spoke up. His eyes narrowed as he leaned in closer, speaking almost at a whisper. "She has been consorting with a beast."

"What are you on about?" Baldric rolled his eyes and fought back a grin. This priest sounded like a frightened child describing the monsters hiding under his bed. Though, perhaps it was best not to wave off every concern with derision. He rubbed his eyes to regain his composure. "What beast?"

"These are the same unfounded rumors that were spread about her father," Irfan interjected. Piet scoffed and waved him off. Irfan turned toward Zuan. "And you only agree with him because she refused your courtship."

"It *is* a devil of incomprehensible evil. We have to put an end to this malice before it threatens our way of life," Piet said, ignoring Irfan's concern. "We cannot allow this corruption to spread."

Zuan's eyes lit up, and he puffed out his chest.

"I will do the honors," Zuan added, placing his hand on the hilt of his sword.

"You most certainly will not," Baldric shot back, scowling. "Look at the two of you. Grown men, afraid of an orphan girl. Who, mind you, is probably grieving the loss of her family. I will speak with her myself."

"My lord, that would be imprudent," Irfan said, reaching out toward Baldric. "The lord of the manor does not handle such things. It would show you a commoner."

Baldric sighed. "My blood doesn't put me above anyone else."

"The laws of your father are quite clear in the matter." Zuan pushed Irfan aside and placed himself within inches of Baldric's face. "We are well within our rights to expel her from the village, and if she does not comply, the sword will suffice."

Baldric stepped around him. "Seems rather extreme. I find a simple conversation can clear up all sorts of misunderstandings."

"That is too dangerous! She should be put to the sword now!" Piet slammed his fist on a nearby table. "The law is also clear on how to handle those who seek out evil, as are the scriptures. We cannot allow her to live."

Baldric rubbed his eyes. There was no reason to be found here. Only a show of strength and power would avert their bloodlust.

"As you said, this is my manor, my land, my world." Baldric stepped up to Piet and Zuan. "You two would be wise to remember that. I will address the issue with her and that will be the end of it. If you push the matter further, I will be forced to take action against you. Is that clear?"

"You don't have the power," Zuan objected.

"Test me and find out," Baldric's reply was cold as he moved toward Zuan. His nose came within inches of the bailiff's. "Now, how do I find her?"

Baldric headed down the snowy hill and into the small village. The square sat at one end of the village, closest to the manor. On the far end was the small chapel. Baldric followed Zuan's instructions as he made his way through the village. Most of the wooden houses were small and dug into the ground for insulation. While the grazing fields for the cows were located just outside the village, most of the houses were grouped together. Their straw mats—which covered the houses from the top of their gabled roofs down to the ground—made it appear as if the village consisted solely of giant bales of hay. What broke the illusion was the pillars of smoke that rose out of each house.

He arrived at a small cottage, which was set further down a rough path between the chapel and the square. The house overlooked the Coldstill River, which twisted its way into the forest. The winter cold had frozen much of the water.

Baldric kicked the snow off his boots and knocked on the door.

"Go away," a woman's sharp voice ordered from within. "I'm done entertaining you for one lifetime."

"I don't believe you've entertained me at all," Baldric answered back. He didn't wait for her to answer, and instead slowly cracked open the door. He poked his head inside. The smell of musty books and smoke met him. "I am Baldric, the new lord of the manor. May I come in?"

"No." Seraphina shot up from her table, dropping her quill to the wooden floor as she rushed toward the door.

Baldric ignored her answer and entered any way. He held up his hands, showing he meant her no harm. He left the door open wide, hoping that would ease her nerves. He was already pushing boundaries as it was. No need to frighten her to death.

"I see you don't listen," Seraphina scoffed. She stepped back, being careful not to trample any of the books under her feet. She positioned herself on the far side of the lit mason stove that took up most of the opposite wall. Her back was toward a door leading to another room.

He was taken aback by her beauty. She was a tall, curvy woman with raven hair, dark eyes, and pale skin. Her eyes glittered with fear and her hands quivered as they hovered near a fire poker. Despite her fear, she was captivating, and he had to stop himself from staring too hard.

"So I've been told." Baldric's response was dry, but a smile tugged at the corner of his lips. He squatted low to make himself appear less threatening. Or at least, he hoped. It seemed to work as she moved her hand away from the poker. "I'm sorry. I don't mean to frighten you."

The small house was a mess. Papers were strewn about. Piles of books were shoved into every corner, while others sat open on the floor. He picked up a large book from the nearest pile and thumbed through its pages.

"A bit of light reading, I see," he teased with a grin. He set the tome gently back on the pile, before aligning them straight so as to not topple over.

"Make whatever snide comments you want," Seraphina huffed, crossing her arms in front of her chest. "I am aware of who you are, and I will not be intimidated."

"Sorry if I offended." Baldric stood and backed up to the open door.

He crossed the threshold so that he was outside. She stepped over the papers and books and marched toward the entrance. He held out his hand to prevent her from slamming the door in his face. Though he had grown used to entering wherever he pleased, he should have thought better of his forcefulness in this instance.

"What is it you want?" Seraphina asked, grabbing the door. Baldric clenched his jaw and braced himself for her to slam it on his arm.

"My steward informs me you haven't paid your rent in some time." He inched his foot forward to hopefully catch the door before it broke his arm.

"And you're here to collect your due?" Seraphina scowled, her plump lips turning down.

Baldric shook his head. "No, I have no intention of pressing the matter. I understand you recently lost your family. I think a bit of leniency will rectify the due. You don't owe me anything. I will see to it you aren't bothered again."

Seraphina opened her mouth as if to argue, but then she froze. She stared at him for a long moment, looking for some hint of deceit in his eyes. Finally, she released a sigh.

"That's... most unexpected," Seraphina said, loosening her grip.

"I heard some distressing rumors." Baldric scratched his head. He was unsure of the most tactful way to discuss this, but since it needed to be addressed, perhaps the direct route was the best. "They said you were consorting with dark magic."

She scoffed and paced around the center of the room, shaking her head and muttering to herself.

"Those fools wouldn't know magic if it struck them in the rear." She stopped and turned toward Baldric. Her deep brown eyes met his. Her nose wrinkled as her eyes narrowed. "Is that your true purpose for being here?"

Baldric sighed and scratched his head. "You really don't want to drop your defenses, do you?"

"The cleric has given me far too few reasons to do so."

"My true purpose is to check on your wellbeing. I heard you were grieving and being harassed and wanted to help. I am also concerned if there is any danger that poses a risk to the rest of the village. As a leader, I would be remiss to overlook these concerns, no matter how unwarranted they may be."

She smirked and motioned him to enter as she retook her seat at the table. Baldric glanced around the room, but there were no other chairs to sit in. At least none that were free from journals and books. He approached the stone stove and pushed aside a large kettle to make room to sit. She turned sideways in her chair, throwing her arm over the short back and leaned against it.

"What vile things has the cleric whispered in your ear?"

"Something about you communing with a beast." Baldric smiled. "I take it you own a cat?"

"A beast?" Seraphina asked, taken aback. She let out a small snicker.

"I believe Father Piet's exact word was 'devil,'" Baldric clarified, smiling. "I mean, I've studied at university, I've studied at monastery, I've even studied at a second and third university. Never once met a devil. And this local priest in the middle of nowhere says one is communing with a beautiful girl with an angelic name. How could I resist?"

"It's just Sera." She smiled back through blushed cheeks. "And here I thought they only offered etiquette lessons to would be princes."

"Understanding the intricacies of a proper place setting is no small feat, I assure you."

Sera laughed. "Indeed."

She regained her composure and eyed him inquisitively. "I wonder what other surprises you hold. Tell me, Mr. Baldric, what do you know of what lies beyond the veil?"

"The veil?" Baldric raised an eyebrow and leaned toward her.

"As I suspected. It remains an unknown even among the most educated. My father only gained awareness through his advisor." She stood from her chair and approached him. She took the black kettle and placed it on the table before sitting beside him. "Our world is but one of many worlds. Our knowledge is limited by what we see before us. If we can learn from these other worlds, think of the advances we could make in science, medicine, agriculture. We could create a new age of understanding and enlightenment."

Baldric squinted as he tried to follow along.

"You speak of the Three Realms?" The Three Realms were separated by magic and ruled by the Guardian. Each realm was appointed a ruler who was given the title of sage, like Baldric's father.

"Hardly." Sera shook her head. She stood and paced back and forth as she explained. "Our world was divided into three separate realities, held apart in space and time, but occupying the same speck within the cosmos. Beyond our own limited perspective of the universe lies universes beyond counting, held apart by the veil."

"I don't know if I understand." Baldric stood and approached her.

"Think of the Realms as this house. Each realm represents a different room," she explained. Her motions became more energetic as she scurried about, educating him on this new subject. "You could create another realm by adding walls and creating another room. Or you could even build onto the house. But it is all the same house.

"The dimensions and alternate realities are like completely separate houses. It's as if we are newborns going outside for the first time and seeing how grand the world is. Infinite possibilities."

She stopped in her tracks. Her mood suddenly somber.

"This was my father's research, and the reason he and my mother were murdered."

Baldric's eyes narrowed. No one mentioned her parents had been murdered, only that they had died. Seemed an odd detail to omit.

"This sounds both enticing and dangerous. You should proceed with caution."

"A wise sentiment," Sera agreed. Glee returned to her face as she seized his hands in her own and pulled him to his feet. Her hands were warm and soft. "Would you like to meet him?"

"Your father?" Baldric took a step back but held on to her. He eyed her up and down. While she looked sane enough, it was not always easy to tell by appearances alone.

She laughed. "No, my father's advisor."

Baldric's eyebrows furrowed. Was this the beast in question?

"Show me."

Baldric followed her into the back room, stepping over the various research notes scattered about. Beakers filled with strange liquids lined the countertops in this room. Each wall was covered with slates, which were filled with scribbles and a seemingly endless array of numbers. They approached a table on the far wall. Sera lifted a black velvet cloth off a glass ball. Inky mist circled in the ball, forming a spinning vortex. A single eye opened in the center of the vortex.

Baldric jumped back and stared at the eye. The eye simply stared back, unblinking.

"Baldric, meet Sokaris," Sera said, motioning to the eye.

"What is that?" Baldric asked, feeling a morbid sense of curiosity despite the alarming nature of the creature.

"A being from another world."

Sera stepped toward the eye. She turned and faced Baldric. Their eyes met, and he felt lost in her gaze.

"At least, its projection." Sera paused and turned toward Sokaris. "Don't worry, he is a friend. Perhaps you can say hello."

"You want me to —" A sharp pain shot through Baldric's skull. He grabbed his head as images and thoughts filled his mind. The images were scattered and difficult to discern—a series of floating islands hovering over a black abyss, flashes of light, and knowledge beyond his own. Baldric gasped and fell to his knees.

"What was that?"

"The first time is quite intense," Sera soothed, kneeling beside him. "I should have warned you."

"I saw his world and felt his curiosity."

"That's how he communicates," Sera explained. She took hold of his arm and helped him to his feet. "His language is far beyond ours, though we can perceive glimpses into what he is communicating."

"I see. He told me... He wants to exchange knowledge." Baldric gazed at the unblinking eye. "He wants to understand... emotions?"

"That is what I gather as well," Sera said with a nod. "He wants to trade knowledge of the infinite cosmos from far beyond the veil and the many worlds for understanding of our emotions."

A realization struck him.

"He's never felt them," Baldric surmised.

"Exactly," Sera said. "Much like we are incapable of understanding his language, he is incapable of feeling human emotions. From what I gather, he is the equivalent of what we would call a god in his reality, though he would never admit this. As mortals, we would be unable to comprehend or even stand in the presence of his true form. Instead, he has explored the cosmos through tears in the veil, forming avatars within orbs like this."

"He then gains the knowledge of whatever new world he is exploring and enriches them with his own." Baldric rubbed his brow. He cupped her hands in his. "What secrets have you learned?"

Baldric followed Sera through her cottage. She showed him stacks of notes and scribbles she had written down, detailing the many worlds and secrets Sokaris had revealed to her. He could do nothing but marvel at the wonders she showed him. She had written tome after tome of mathe-

matical theory far beyond his understanding, medical prac-
tices and remedies which would elongate the human lifes-
pan, technology and engineering of machines that bor-
dered on magic, and of course, real magic, which turned
dreams into reality. With just a brief glimpse of each field,
he was enraptured.

"Would you care to stay for dinner?" she asked, as the day
waned on. "I must admit, I've enjoyed your company. I've
never had anyone to talk to like this before."

"Would it be possible?" he asked. "I wouldn't be intruding?"

"I wouldn't mind your intrusion so much. Besides, there
is a lot we can learn from each other."

He stayed with her, studying and exploring the myster-
ies of the universe. Hours became days, days turned into
weeks, and weeks passed into months. To facilitate their
research, he moved her into the manor with him, along
with all her notes and instruments. Soon, the library was
filled with experiments and tinkerings. Neither of them
fully understood most of the concepts, but Sokaris was patient, explaining through visions just how intricate reality
could be.

Out of all their research, Sera was most fascinated with
mathematics and astronomy. With Baldric's funding, she
was able to take her research further than ever. She would
spend hours gazing at the heavens with telescopes of her
own design, which surpassed any Baldric had seen in the
royal universities. He, on the other hand, was determined

to create a self-moving machine like the ones he had seen in so many other worlds. The key to create basic functionality seemed to rely on harnessing steam to generate motion.

They bonded quickly. As a child, Baldric had moved around and traveled so much, he never had much in the way of friends. He was never treated as an equal among his peers—always as a prince. While it was hardly the worst way to be treated, it was still isolating and lonely.

Likewise, Sera had been ostracized and scorned by the village. Even before the rumors spread about her, few saw the appeal in higher learning, and she was often treated as an outcast.

They found comfort in each other and a comradery that neither had experienced before. Within a few months of living together, those feelings of friendship blossomed into romance, which only grew stronger over time. It was her intelligence and curiosity that he admired most about her. She had a never-ending hunger for gaining new knowledge. As Sokaris showed them wonders and their knowledge grew, so did their feelings for one another.

Baldric wondered just what Sokaris got out of their arrangement. He had stated he wanted to learn about human emotions, yet he never asked questions. He simply observed and provided answers to their inquiries. The only question he ever asked them occurred the day after Baldric and Sera first made love. It was a single question with no follow up, and he never brought it up again.

"Do you know you've been smiling for nearly two hours?" Sokaris had asked Sera.

Honestly, Baldric found it more unnerving than anything. Perhaps they were *his* test subjects. While Sokaris didn't speak with words, some of the thoughts and information that were projected into their minds could be interpreted and assigned to spoken language—others less so. This was the only time those thoughts posed an inquiry.

Even more so, the question was so very human in nature. Sokaris had never seemed to grasp the concept of time before—having lived since before the beginning of his universe. Then again, perhaps it was simply their human minds misinterpreting his thoughts.

A year passed, and Sokaris never asked another question. He just watched while they continued their research and fell deeper in love.

Baldric and Sera were nearly inseparable. As the early winter came again, they found themselves finding warmth in each other's embrace more often. He found no matter how many times they were together, it never was enough. Often, they would leave their research to enjoy one another's bodies in hidden corners of the manor. Their exploration of each other was just as thorough as their studies, and their love grew as vast as the infinite cosmos.

* * *

Baldric entered the great room where Piet was waiting for him. He closed the door behind him to trap what little heat was in the room and headed straight for the fire. He tossed a log into the fireplace and warmed his hands.

"Father Piet. How may I help you?" Baldric turned toward the cleric and extended his warmed hand for the cleric to shake.

Piet stared down at Baldric's outstretched hand, but did not take it.

"It is not proper for that woman to live in your manor."

"It is *my* manor," Baldric said, dropping his hand to his side. "We've been over this before. I can offer quarter to anyone I choose. If this is all you've come to say, we can avoid repeating ourselves and you can leave."

"People are talking!" Piet insisted, eyes growing wide.

"Let them!" Baldric snapped back. "I have no concern for rumors and gossip."

"It is more than that," Piet said, grasping both of Baldric's shoulders. Baldric clenched his jaw and glared at the old priest, who was now intruding in his house and belittling his love. "Her father was a great philosopher, but he made a pact with a devil. It corrupted him and threatened to destroy our village. That same evil flows in her veins."

"I assure you, her veins and yours are filled with the same substance," Baldric said, pulling away from his grip. "Perhaps you are unaware, but some of those rumors about us are true. You would be wise to remember that."

Baldric turned for the door.

"She is malicious and untrustworthy, but she is beautiful, and you are young," Piet rushed forward, catching up to step in front of Baldric. "She believes you to be malleable and will use you to her own ends. Trust me, this relationship is toxic and will be the end of you and this village."

"Says the man who is celibate and has never experienced love like this." Baldric rolled his eyes and stepped around Piet. "You've overstayed your welcome. Please leave."

"You gave quarter to a woman who refuses to work," Piet reminded. "Who hasn't paid rent. The scriptures are clear. Everyone must work and labor for their food."

"I don't." Baldric turned to face Piet. He pressed his finger into the cleric's chest. "Neither do you."

"You are royalty." Piet pushed Baldric's hand away. "Your family works to provide guidance to the kingdom. And I am an emissary of the gods. I bring spirituality to the masses."

"And she's bringing knowledge."

"At the cost of both your souls!" Piet spat. The priest wrapped his arm around Baldric's shoulders. "I'm telling you this for your own good. That woman is evil. I know you're stricken by her beauty. I do not fault you for your carnal desires, but it is nothing more than a trap. If you must, finish with her, then cast her out."

Baldric clenched his teeth and his nostrils flared as he stared down the priest.

"You are out of line." He wrenched Piet's wrist free from his shoulder and dragged him toward the door. "I've been accommodating and patient with you. I suggest you leave and never speak of this matter again. Or I will see to it you are removed from your duties."

"No, it is you who is out of line!" Piet shouted, rending his arm free from Baldric's grasp. "For countless generations, the clergy has advised your family. I may just be a lowly priest, but my word carries just as much authority as yours. If not more so."

"Your authority means nothing to me." Baldric glared at the priest; his brow furrowed. "I come from a line of kings."

"What is a king to a god?" Piet hissed, staring back. "I speak for the gods themselves. Even the Guardian serves as their champion. Who do you think carries more clout? I assure you; the gods and the Guardian would side with the church over your family. If you threaten me again, I will bring down the wrath of the gods upon you. But if you allow me to deal with this witch, I will guarantee your entry into heaven."

Baldric shook his head.

"This conversation is going nowhere. I grow weary. Shut the door on your way out." He turned and walked out of the side door and into the hallway.

Piet moved toward the door, but just before he stepped through, he looked back at Baldric.

"Don't allow yourself to be corrupted by that vile woman." Then he was gone.

Baldric ignored his words and stomped up the stairs to his study, shutting and locking the door behind him. He collapsed in his desk chair and rubbed his hand through his hair. He had tried to be diplomatic, but it led him nowhere. Piet kept making the same points over and over, but each time, he was becoming more impassioned and forceful. He had never threatened him before.

Baldric turned his head and stared at Sokaris, whose single eye watched him from his orb. Baldric nodded as Sokaris's thoughts entered his mind.

"He speaks through action. He is afraid." Sokaris seemed to say. Baldric gazed into the floating eye. How much of this emotion was he beginning to understand? The inky black mist swirled in the orb as Sokaris gazed back into Baldric. "And so are you."

* * *

"We have to do something about this witch." Piet paced back and forth across the chapel's chancel, while Zuan looked on from the front row pew, stroking his chin. "She has seduced the young lord and is corrupting our village with her stench. He has fallen prey to her, and soon we will all suffer."

"We've discussed this before." Zuan shook his head. "We eliminated her father when he became a nuisance. We should do the same with her."

"I agree," Piet said, stopping in his tracks and facing the bailiff. "Though I fear we will be unable to make a move against her so long as she has bewitched the prince."

"He gave up his birthright," Zuan reminded. "The king doesn't want him around. I doubt the boy has enough clout to cause us much harm."

"You might be right." Piet folded his arms as he pondered the thought. "Still, I would feel better if we broke her grasp."

"What do you have in mind?" Zuan asked.

"We gather the deacons of the church and hold a tribunal," Piet said, beginning to pace again. "If she is found guilty, we can force her to break her spell."

"I wouldn't rely on the deacons," Zuan said. "Too many of them are infatuated with her beauty. They would be too easily swayed."

"I believe you once courted her. Did you not?" Piet shot him a side eyed glance. "Perhaps it is you who is too infatuated with her."

"That was a long time ago." Zuan averted his gaze, staring at the wooden slats of the floor. "Before she fell in league with devils."

"The deacons are all pious, like myself." Piet slammed his fist down into his palm as if it were a gavel. "I can show them how this will impact their entry into heaven. They will come to the right conclusion, and we will finally have this matter settled and behind us."

"And the boy?"

"The deacons and I will force her to release him from her magic before she dies, and if not—well, I doubt anyone would mind his disappearance."

CHAPTER TWO

BALDRIC ROLLED OVER TO Sera, wrapping his arm around her. She sighed and turned toward him. She kissed him gently on the neck as they embraced.

"I truly am the luckiest man alive," Baldric said. He leaned back, placing his head on his pillow, and closed his eyes.

"Going to sleep so soon?" she asked.

"Soon?" Baldric opened one eye. "We've been up for hours. It's getting late."

"But the stars are so pretty this time of night."

He groaned and draped his arms over his face.

"Don't go to sleep," she protested, hitting him with her pillow. "There is still so much to learn."

"It appears I haven't exhausted you thoroughly enough." He smiled and kissed her forehead. "We should get some rest. There's always tomorrow."

"You've seen what I've seen," Sera said. "I fear our lives aren't long enough to study it all. There will be some things we will never know."

"If you learn too much, your head will burst," Baldric teased. "I'll sleep now, and learn later."

"If that is what you wish." Sera pulled back the covers and got out of bed. She picked up her clothes, which she had hung over the back of a chair, and began dressing herself.

"You need sleep too," Baldric reminded, sitting upright.

"There's not enough time." She pulled her shirt over her head. "We are so close to creating a new age. One that isn't predicated on fear and superstition. How can I rest now?"

He adored her optimism and passion. She had such hopes and dreams for the future. They weren't even to benefit herself but to create a better age for all humanity. In some ways, she was the opposite of him. He had long ago given up on improving his father's kingdom. It was an impossible task. Yet, here she was, firmly believing she could make the impossible possible.

"Are you going to accomplish all that in one night?"

"I am a fast learner." Sera smiled. "That's what Sokaris says, anyway."

Baldric's smile faded. Perhaps it was ridiculous to be jealous of a god, but emotions could not be controlled, only reacted too. He wasn't even sure if Sokaris could express love or desire for a mortal. He somehow seemed beyond human understanding and feelings. However, Sokaris did favor her over him, preferring to communicate with her when the two were together.

It didn't matter either way. Baldric didn't own Sera, and he trusted in their relationship.

"If we are to bring about this new age," Sera said, sitting down next to him on the bed. "It would be beneficial to have your father aid us in our quest. Once our studies are complete, of course."

"I'm not so sure he would be interested in anything I have to say." Baldric clenched his jaw.

He was an only child, and would be his father's sole successor had he not given up his claim to the throne. Baldric never felt qualified for the throne and, thus, refused to be king.

Because of his abdication, he'd been banished to Crescentwood. His cousin, the new successor to the throne, felt threatened by Baldric's presence at Drakon. The last words his father spoke to him weren't simply of disappointment, they were words of anger and resentment.

"After everything we've learned, why not return?" Sera asked. "Even just as an advisor."

"I would be a threat to the new king when he ascends," Baldric explained. "And I am not qualified to be king. The circumstances of my birth have no bearing on my leadership abilities. I cannot wield supreme power simply due to who my parents are."

"Isn't that how kings are decided?" Sera asked.

"How many worlds have we seen where better leaders are chosen from the people? How many worlds where the lines of kings have been corrupted and exploited the masses? If anything, this exploration has shown my decision to be the right one."

"You are probably right, but the line of kings will continue with or without you," Sera said. "The only difference is, you will now have no say in the future of the kingdom."

He sighed. "It's something to think about, at least."

She clasped her hand over his. "I am proud of the decision you made. It took a lot of courage and determination. We all have to find our own path. We will do the same to bring about the new age."

"Thank you."

He stroked the side of her face. Her fair skin was smooth and soft. The touch of her skin electrified his body. She leaned forward and pressed her lips against his. His world was complete.

* * *

She headed to the library while he drifted off to sleep. Sokaris watched her as she entered. She smiled as his thoughts bounced in her head.

"Your essence is strongest after being with him," Sokaris seemed to say. "And he is the same."

"It's called love," Sera said, laughing.

She always spoke aloud to him. She was uncertain if he had the ability to read her thoughts. He seemed capable of deciphering what she was thinking, but it was unclear if he was determining that through body language or telepathy.

She approached her telescope, which sat on a stand near the large bay window. The window was the clearest in the manor. Baldric had it specially made for her over the summer, so she wouldn't be exposed to the cold during the long winter. He had designed it to using two panes of glass to provide insulation from the cold.

Sera gazed through the telescope up at the stars. It was hard to fathom just how large the universe was. The earth was a speck of dust drifting through space. Despite the sheer size of the cosmos, the universe was trivial when compared to the limitless number of realities beyond the void. It really highlighted how insignificant the struggles of humanity were in the grand scheme of things. There was no power in the cosmos which was going to solve humanity's problems. Only humans could do that.

"I see your wickedness knows no limits."

The voice behind her made her jump. She turned to find Piet entering the library. He shut the door behind him.

"How did you get in here?"

"The steward let me in," Piet answered simply, locking the double doors. "I told him I had an important matter to discuss with you."

"I want nothing to do with you." Sera backed away from him, bumping into the telescope.

She fought against her trembling legs and reached behind her and gripped its stand. If need be, she could swing it like a club. The telescope might break, but the metal frame should give her enough time to escape.

"Evil never wishes to be in the presence of good," Piet sneered.

He reached down and picked up a book off the floor. He held it outstretched in front of him, only gripping it with two fingers as if it were diseased.

"Nonsense such as this is only good for kindling." He smirked and dropped the book. Its pages fluttered as it fell and collided with the wooden floor.

"Your limited understanding betrays your character." She swung the telescope free from its stand and pointed its tip at him. "Don't come any closer. I know you're responsible for my father's death."

"Where's Baldric?" Piet asked, stepping toward her.

Sera backed away, her heart pounding in her chest. She had dreaded this day for nearly two years. When he would finally come for her. "Why should I tell you?"

He stepped within striking distance.

"You are to come with me." He smirked. "Unless you intend to beg like your father."

Her knuckles turned white. He wanted her to fight back. It would give him an excuse.

Could she run? Sokaris tugged at her mind. She nodded in agreement as flashes of blood and ash filled her thoughts. But she already knew. Piet was here for her life.

"If you resist me," Piet said, brushing aside the telescope. "I'll inflict your fate upon Baldric as well. If you care for him, you won't resist."

Sokaris screamed in her mind. He wanted her to run and fight back. He wanted to tear open the veil and save her—but even he knew the truth. She was alone in this dispute.

Her fear might have overtaken her then, but she couldn't let them hurt the man she loved. She couldn't allow them to kill Baldric in the same way they had murdered her parents. The way they were going to murder *her*.

Sera fought back the tears forming in her eyes as a gasp slipped past her lips. She wasn't going to give him the pleasure.

"Sokaris," she said in her mind. "Take care of Baldric."

She nodded and dropped the telescope. It clamored to the floor. She gathered what little courage she had left. "I won't resist."

Piet smiled and placed his hand on her shoulder. "Good. Follow me."

She followed him out of the manor and into the snowy night. A group of men waited in the courtyard—deacons of the church as well as Zuan. His eyes landed on her and he smiled. She glared back. It wasn't so long ago he'd been courting her. She had turned him down. Now he clearly wanted her dead.

What a weak man.

Piet motioned her to walk. The group surrounded and guided her. Their footprints crunched in the snow as they made their way into the forest.

* * *

Pain shot through Baldric's skull. He launched himself out of bed. Images of blood and ash flashed in his mind—an icy forest and the frozen river, stained red. Just as suddenly as they started, the images stopped. He sat on the edge of his bed, gripping the sides of his head, his chest heaving.

Sera was in danger.

No, it was more than that.

Baldric raced out of his bedchamber and burst into the library. His blood froze. Sera's telescope lay broken on the floor. His gaze shot toward Sokaris and the unblinking eye. Sokaris's eye glistened in the misty vortex. He broke eye contact and turned his gaze away from Baldric. His eye closed, and the black mist vanished, leaving the orb empty.

Sokaris was gone.

Baldric swallowed hard. His hands trembled. He couldn't accept this. He wouldn't.

He spun on his heels and darted out the door.

"Irfan!" Baldric shouted as he ran down the stairs. "Where's Sera?"

"I believe Father Piet requested her presence," Irfan responded. "I am unsure why."

"You let him in? Do you know what you've done?" Baldric shoved past the steward.

He didn't stop for his coat or shoes. He simply rushed out of the manor and into the cold.

"My lord!" Irfan called out. "You'll freeze!"

Baldric didn't stop or even hear the warning. He knew where she was. Sokaris had told him. He couldn't allow himself to believe the rest of his message, not yet.

The dawn light broke through the treetops. Baldric's bare feet pounded in the snow and frost as he ran towards the river. The cold stabbed into his skin, numbing his extremities. His feet reddened and burned, but he didn't care. He only halted his pace as he reached the riverbed. His heart stopped, frozen like the river before him.

The white snow was painted red with blood and dotted with bits of flesh. A heap of meat lay face down on top of the frozen river. Baldric fell to his knees beside the body. He cradled Sera in his arms. She was barely recognizable. Her face had been cut and her eyes gouged out.

Baldric let out an earth-shattering cry as he held her tight. Hot tears streamed down his frozen face. He kissed her bloody forehead.

"Come back to me," he whispered.

"By the gods!" Irfan said, approaching. He averted his gaze, refusing to look at the carnage. "What have they done? Whatever grievances they had; they had no right to do this!"

Baldric stared up at the man, but didn't say anything. What was there to say? What words could describe the slew of emotions running through him?

"Why would the gods allow such madness to happen?" Irfan asked, his face white.

Baldric wiped at his tears, streaking blood across his face.

"The gods had nothing to do with this."

Irfan stepped closer and draped a coat around Baldric.

"We should take her back to the manor. We can clean her up and prepare the funeral rites."

Baldric ripped the cloak off his shoulders. He wrapped Sera within the heavy wool fabric and lifted her body up.

"Let me help you," Irfan urged, reaching out to Baldric.

He pulled away from him and hugged Sera tight.

"I've got her."

Baldric carried her back to Crescentwood. He placed her body on the sofa in the great room in front of the fire.

"I don't want to live without you," Baldric mumbled, sitting across from Sera's body. "The world is lesser without you in it."

"We should get you cleaned up, sir," Irfan said.

Baldric shook his head as he knelt beside the sofa. He stared, unblinking, at Sera's corpse, still wrapped in his cloak.

"Bring me my boots."

Irfan hesitated before speaking.

"What are you going to do?"

"I am the lord of this land." Baldric stood to his feet, but still didn't take his eyes off Sera. "I will not allow such treachery to go unpunished."

"Father Piet is well respected," Irfan warned, retrieving Baldric's boots from the nearby cupboard. "Confronting him could be dangerous."

"I am the king's son," Baldric reminded him, snatching the boots from his outstretched hands. "Confronting *me* is dangerous."

He shoved on his boots. Still not bothering with a coat, he marched to the town. The sun was fully up. The deacons and elders of the town would be at church preparing for morning service.

Good. He could expose the father's crimes to the whole village.

Baldric marched toward the sanctuary. It was a small building with a gabled roof that extended to the ground. Like most buildings in the village, a straw mat covered the roof for insulation.

A carved sunburst—the symbol of the Triune Gods—sat in front of the chapel, like a sign showing the building's purpose. A lantern, hung with a chain upon a pole, flickered above the wooden sunburst. Baldric scoffed. The gods were the bringers of peace, yet that didn't stop its members from committing great acts of evil.

Baldric charged toward the large double doors and threw them open. The men inside gasped and turned in their pews to face him. They were scattered amongst the chapel's red cushioned pews. The light from the fireplace and the scattered lanterns cast shadows upon their faces. They stared, stunned, seeing the lord of the manor setting foot inside the chapel for the first time. Baldric locked eyes with Piet and stepped down the aisle toward him.

"Tell them what you did!" Baldric demanded, his feet thumping on the red carpet as he stomped toward the cleric. "Or should I?"

"By all means," Piet motioned to the deacons. "We simply followed the commands of the gods. Do you not see this? Or have you too been corrupted by the beast?"

"You murdered an innocent woman!" Baldric shouted.

"She was a witch!" Zuan yelled back, his face red as he stood from a middle pew. "She would have brought corruption to us all."

"You were involved as well?" Baldric's brow furrowed as he glared at his bailiff.

One deacon stood and moved toward the front.

"We all agreed it was best for the village," he said. "It was unanimous."

"How did you think I would respond?" Baldric asked. His hand shot to his face as he tried to process how so many people could condone this murder. "This is my land, my kingdom. My word is law, and I will hold you all responsible for her death."

"Don't delude yourself," Zuan spat, sliding his way through the pew and out into the aisle. "You are the banished son of the king. You gave up any power you once had with your birthright."

"My father will hear of this treachery," Baldric promised, shooting daggers with his eyes.

"Your father sent you to live in the frozen wastes with us." Piet said, his voice calm as he clasped his hands together in feigned humility. "Do you think he cares about what happens to you?"

"Killing you would probably resolve any future issues of succession," Zuan added. He pulled back his waistcoat, revealing the smallsword strapped to his belt. "We would be doing him a favor. Your manor, your title, your life. You only have these things because we allow it. Anything could happen to you, and the only thing your father would ever be aware of is what we tell him. If we so chose, we could end you, and no one would know or care."

Baldric clenched his fists. His eyes shot back and forth between Zuan and Piet. His heart sank. There was some truth to his words. Likely, his death would only be seen as little more than an insult to the king. But there was a second truth hiding in the subtext. If they truly believed there would be no consequences, he would already be dead. He still had power in this game of life and death, which they so desired to play. He would make them regret that.

The deacons in the pews murmured amongst themselves. They weren't quite as bold as Piet and Zuan, but their tacit agreement with them had already confirmed where they stood. Baldric's ears perked up as he heard their words.

"The witch got what she deserved."

"Here, here."

"We should have done it ages ago."

"We won't make the same mistake again."

"Who cares what he says? He has no real power."

Baldric seethed as rage boiled inside him. He truly was alone in acknowledging the horror of what they'd done.

Piet spoke again, drawing the eyes of everyone in the room back to him.

"Even the king knows when to bow to the clergy." He descended the chancel and approached Baldric. "He wouldn't dare move against our decree. We exterminated a witch. Nothing more. That is the truth of this world."

"Not anymore," Baldric snarled.

"Huff all you want," Piet said, coming within inches of Baldric's face. He smirked. "It's nothing but bluster without power. Even the king is subservient to the Guardian—the Prophet of Talus—and I am one of his priests! Believe me, one of us holds real power. The other does not."

Zuan shifted, placing his hand on the hilt of his sword. Baldric eyed him. He couldn't fight against a seasoned veteran. He couldn't stand against them. They were stronger and more numerous. Piet was right. If the Guardian heard of this, he would side with his priest. Even if Baldric could convince his father to aid him, all Piet had to do was to appeal to the Guardian, and what little power his father possessed would be stripped away.

Nothing would change.

"I think you should leave," Zuan threatened. "The righteous have worship to prepare for."

Baldric clenched his jaw. He *was* powerless. His father *was* powerless. True power lied in the hands of those who would abuse it, leaving the oppressed as victims. He averted his eyes and stared at the ground. "I understand. That's how the world is."

He turned and shuffled towards the exit.

"Shut the door on your way out," Piet called.

Baldric complied, stepping out into the bright day. He turned and stared up at the sunburst and the flickering lantern. His arms dangled by his side, and his legs trembled and grew numb. There was no justice in this world. Sera's murder would go unpunished. Every word they said was true. Baldric took a deep breath. The air filled his lungs and chipped at the boulder crushing his spirit.

It didn't have to be true.

Not anymore, at least. He had the knowledge given to him by Sokaris. He could build the new age Sera dreamed of. He would fight with every fiber of his being to obtain the power necessary to ensure injustices like this never happened again. There was just one thing he needed to do first.

He returned to Crescentwood Manor, but he didn't enter. He couldn't bear to see her body again. Not like that. Instead, he went to the stables and saddled a horse.

He heard a step on the gravel outside the stable doors.

"My lord." Irfan approached as Baldric mounted the steed. "How did it go? Is everything alright?"

"Take care of Sera," Baldric said, ignoring Irfan's questions. "Make sure she is properly buried."

"What are you going to do?"

Baldric stared past the doors, down the slope toward the village. The new age Sera had so desperately wanted could only come about through power. It was time for him to set upon his destined path.

"I'm going to reclaim my birthright."

He ignored Irfan's stupefied expression and galloped away. The horse's hooves kicked up snow and dirt along the way. He paused at the chapel. He wanted nothing more than to go back in and tell them off. Threaten that he would become king and avenge Sera's death. That he would ensure the church never harmed another innocent again from its corruption.

But he knew it wouldn't do any good.

Worse, they could strike him down on the spot. They would never know of his plans. After all, there was a solid chance he would fail in his endeavor. Everything seemed against him at this point. Even if he succeeded, Sera's murderers may never face justice. Years would pass, and they could scatter to the four corners of the wind.

Images of her bleeding body flashed through his mind.

Wrath boiled within him. He wouldn't allow them to escape. He jumped off the horse and grabbed the lantern and unhooked the chain from which it hung. He marched toward the large double doors and wrapped the chain around the handles, locking them in place. Without a second thought, he threw the lantern at the chapel. It struck the side of the building, bursting into a small blaze, but it was enough. The straw and wood caught fire.

That was all he needed to see. Baldric didn't wait to ensure the rest burned, nor did he stop to watch or gloat.

He threw the lantern, mounted his horse, and rode hard out of the village. It was a long journey to castle Drakon, but rest would have to wait. He wouldn't stop until he had the power to change the world and bring forth the new age Sera dreamed of. As he rode, smoke billowed high into the sky, blackening the air of the village with ash. Baldric didn't see it.

He never looked back.

PART II
A Passional of Scorn

CHAPTER THREE

KING BALDRIC SCOWLED AND gritted his teeth. He leaned forward in his chair, clasping his hands together tight enough to turn his knuckles white. The other leaders of the Three Realms sat together in silence in their red cushioned chairs, contemplating the stratagem before them.

"How can you condone this?" he demanded, breaking the silence. His eyes glared, fixated on the Guardian.

The Immortal Warrior stared back at him from across the room, his chiseled face solemn and still, flanked by his long brown hair and beard. His brown eyes showed no hint of hesitation. Despite the tension among the three sages, the guardian sat calmly, his tall frame slouched in his throne. "We have little choice in the matter."

Baldric bit his lip as he fought back the urge to unleash his fury. There was little use in disagreeing with the Immortal Warrior. As the Undefeated Champion of the Gods—a title he bestowed upon himself—he served as the ultimate arbitrator in all matters within the Three Realms. It wasn't like he didn't earn the title. He battled and fought his way into power over a thousand years ago, and in that time-frame, none had ever been able to stand against his will.

The only way to avoid this atrocity was to change his mind.

"It's a sound strategy," Legato, the Sage of Terra, added before taking a bite of sweet cake.

Baldric scoffed.

Of course Legato would think so. It was his idea. Out of the Three Sages, Legato was always the first to toady to the Guardian. He was the longest serving of the three and controlled the richest and most powerful realm. But it was his leadership that saw Terra torn apart in war. Now he was desperate to fix it, to reclaim his power and station in the eyes of the guardian. Legato smirked, as if he was imparting some sage advice.

A sly smile spread across Legato's face. "After all, why have a war if you're not willing to win it?"

"Why have this war at all!?" Baldric shouted, jumping to his feet, nearly knocking over the tray of food that sat on the table between them. "Just let them be!"

"They attacked first," Sage Zagu of Niwend said, steading the tray.

He reached out and placed his hand on Baldric's, reining him back in. Baldric jerked away and glared down at Zagu, who remained seated. Zagu was the only one Baldric would even consider a friend. They shared a lot of the same ideas and beliefs, but in Baldric's opinion, Zagu had given up. He would challenge the Immortal Warrior when necessary, but if it appeared the argument wasn't going his way, he was always quick to back down from a confrontation.

"That's enough." the Immortal Warrior held up his hands to silence his sages. "No one wants this war, Baldric. However, we cannot allow them to go unheeded. Baldric, please understand, these rebels must be bought into line and quickly. It is the only way to end this war."

Baldric swung his hands around wildly, desperately pleading his case. "Why not simply give them their independence? That's all they desire. The chance to rule themselves out from under your ty—" Baldric stopped himself and dropped into his chair. He cut his eyes toward the large window and stared into the evening sky. He dared not finish and call the guardian a tyrant to his face.

"Under his what?" Legato demanded, standing to his feet, his hand resting firmly on the hilt of his sword. "Finish the sentence. We all know what you're thinking."

"Leave him alone, Legato," Zagu said, waving off Legato's fury.

"Agreed," The Immortal Warrior motioned Legato to re-take his seat by his side. Legato nodded and sat without delay. "Baldric is young and naïve. His idealism is a welcomed addition to this council. However, we cannot simply give in to their demands. If we allow these so called 'Sovereign' nations to betray the treaty *they* signed, and which has stood for over a thousand years, there is no telling what else they might do. It would jeopardize the stability of the Three Realms, and I will die before I allow that to happen."

Baldric sneered. Unlike Ariel the Immortal Warrior, death meant something to him. The Immortal Warrior had lived for thousands of years. He forged the Triune Concordant, conquered the Three Realms, and forced all nations to submit to his rule.

Baldric sunk into his chair, his body stiff and rigid. He couldn't give up. He wouldn't surrender his will the same as Zagu. He just had to be more cunning in his approach.

"Fine, I accept the need to continue this battle, but the methods presented will result in an unacceptable loss of life for *both* sides. Our own men will die needlessly."

"It is the quickest way to break through the Shagin line and crush their spirit," Legato said, rolling his eyes. "We cannot show any weakness at this juncture."

"*Oh, would you shut up?*" Baldric wanted to say but knew better. He cut his eyes toward Legato, shooting daggers. He swallowed hard to push back his anger. "What about the emissary? They requested to meet with us, and we're not even going to hear them out?"

The Immortal Warrior pinched his brow and shook his head. "No, I don't think so. They know they cannot stand against the coalition of the Three Realms. They moved to secure the continent to prevent the arrival of our might, and they failed. Only now that their line has faltered do they wish to parley. I will not abdicate power and negotiate. I will only accept their unconditional surrender and the execution of their leaders."

"You've caged them," Baldric said, his hand flexing in frustration. How could they not see this? "Such demands only result in forcing them to fight beyond what is reasonable. Their options are either fight or death."

"They knew the consequences when they broke the concordant." Legato slammed his hand down on the arm of his chair.

Baldric rolled his eyes. They only broke the concordant when Legato and the Immortal Warrior intervened in the Mylian Civil War and massacred the Koroks—all for the greater good. Or so they said.

"Zagu," the Immortal Warrior said, "What do you think? You have devised some of the most cunning strategies of this war. What alternative tactics can you create?"

"I am of the mind to agree with Baldric," Zagu said, his eyes casting downward. "Though I don't feel comfortable sending so many to die. The Shagin hold the canyons on the far end of the plains. Their magic is formidable and their line is strong. We have the superior forces. We can either send our forces around and attempt to flank them, or cut off their supply lines and wait them out. However, both of those scenarios could take weeks. Long enough for them to be resupplied or reinforcements to arrive."

"That's unacceptable," the Immortal Warrior said. "It is decided. We'll batter the center Shagin line with wave after wave. Preferably, less experienced soldiers from Niwend and Adgul, as they have the least familiarity with fighting in this terrain. We'll save the strength of our best fighters for once we are ready to break through. We'll allow fatigue and exhaustion to defeat them. Once their supplies and strength dwindle, the four of us will lead an all-out offensive with all our forces on all fronts. We will break through the exhausted center line—their forces will scatter and this war will be over."

"How can we condemn our own soldiers like that?" Baldric asked. "We've already lost so much. Forty thousand in three days! And you want to *maximize* that?"

"As you've said, we've lost forty thousand in three days due to the Shagin front alone." Legato glared at him. "We've amassed the largest military force in history, and they've held us at bay with only four thousand Shagin and a paltry force of regular militia."

"That paltry force is nearly half a million," Zagu corrected, leaning forward.

"And we still outnumber them by twelve," the Immortal Warrior added. He picked up his wineglass from the table and swirled the liquid around before downing its contents. "Due to logistical limitations, we can only bring forth a fraction of our numbers to bare at a time."

"They almost routed us yesterday," Legato continued, "and you want to wait until the number of Shagin has *doubled*? The world is watching this battle. If we falter, we can expect more nations to turn to their cause, but if we crush them, we take the victory and their morale."

The Immortal Warrior slammed his hand down onto the arm of his chair. "Enough discussion. I have made my decision. Baldric, is that clear?"

Baldric clenched his jaw, but did not protest.

"Good." The Immortal Warrior stood to his feet. "Prepare your men for battle. Tomorrow, we'll begin to wear down the Shagin line and claim victory."

Baldric stormed out of the meeting. He didn't care what they thought of him. He didn't risk everything to claim the throne to only be another powerless puppet to the guardian.

When he had returned to Drakon—following his banishment to Crescentwood—his father was less than pleased to see him. Baldric still had nightmares about what had happened. The initial return wasn't so bad. There was a lot of yelling and anger, but that was expected. His cousin Randall had already been publicly recognized as the crown prince, and he was not very happy with Baldric's return, either.

They had locked Baldric in the tower of Castle Drakon to await their decision on what to do with him. He didn't have to wait long. A few hours after his imprisonment, his father, cousin, and uncle entered his cell with weapons drawn. He knew they would be angry; he knew Randall would hate him, but he never imagined they would try to kill him.

Unfortunately for them, part of Baldric's education involved learning how to fend off would-be assassins. His cousin and uncle never stood a chance. His father, however, was a different matter. As sage, he had been taught how to harness his spirit energy by the Immortal Warrior, making him resistant to damage. It was a long and brutal fight that only ended when Baldric wore down his father's energy and pushed a dagger into his heart.

With their deaths, there was no one to stop him from assuming the throne. He had accomplished what he set out to do, though it wasn't the way he had intended it. Publicly, their deaths were the work of an assassin, and their untimely demised forced Baldric to return from exile and take the crown he never wanted to wear.

His reign had been built on lies and murder, and it seemed impotence would be its defining characteristic.

Six years had passed since that day, and he still wasn't used to his role. Almost immediately after, war descended upon the Three Realms.

All of Baldric's grand plans had to be set aside to aid the war effort. The new age he promised to bring about for Sera looked more and more fleeting with each passing year. He had been forced to sabotage his own inventions and hide the knowledge he had gained from Sokaris. Baldric's metallurgy, his engineering, even his medicine, was taken from him and weaponized by the Immortal Warrior.

Luckily, despite his proficiency with magic, the Immortal Warrior was quite dense. Without Baldric's knowledge, most of his attempts failed. And Baldric was all too happy to find ways to break his own creations.

It did sadden him to crash the airship, though. He had *"forgotten"* to include a method of descending in the schematics. When the Immortal Warrior asked him to fix the flaw, Baldric *"tried,"* but it was *"beyond"* his knowledge. He simply failed to mention the finished model he had stored within his shipyard. Although, at this point, it did seem increasingly unlikely it would ever get the opportunity to soar.

"My lord," Ekene said as Baldric stomped down the halls, "you looked troubled."

"You could say that." Baldric rubbed his hand through his dark hair as he stopped in front of his retainer. "We have to find a way to stop this war."

"I've done as you've asked," Ekene said, leaning towards Baldric and dropping his voice down to that of a whisper. "I've contacted the Shagin emissary. I take it by your demeanor, the Immortal Warrior has refused the meeting."

"Yeah." Baldric sighed and nodded, his mind racing with the magnitude of the task before him. He rubbed his hand through his brown hair. "Which means it's up to me to end this war before another atrocity occurs."

"Won't this be seen as treason?" Ekene looked around frantically to make sure no one was listening.

"Yes, I'm sure it will be." Baldric said, nodding in agreement. "But I don't see another way out of this mess we're in. If anyone finds out, you knew nothing of my actions. I did this on my own."

"Thank you, my lord."

"No, thank you for your help." Baldric placed his hand on Ekene's shoulder. "I know this isn't easy for you, but with any luck, our efforts won't be in vain."

Baldric turned and made his way towards his quarters to prepare for the meeting. He had no idea what he would say when he met the Shagin emissary, nor how he would convince them to surrender given the circumstances. Even if they did agree, what would he do then? The Immortal Warrior was hellbent on making an example of them. It seemed a peaceful resolution might already be beyond reach. But he had to try.

Baldric snuck out of the encampment in the dark of night. He gathered a small group of his soldiers to accompany him in case he was walking into a trap. It was only a token force, but hopefully it would be enough to deter any aggression. He headed east, away from the plains and into the nearby canyons. It was a long trek, which meant he wouldn't be getting much sleep tonight, but that was a concern for later.

He approached the meeting place, marked by two braziers. The flames flickered and cast shadows on the canyon rocks. Two young women stepped out from the shadows. Shagin, no doubt. They were pretty and youthful—early twenties, if he had to guess. Just old enough to have begun fighting at the beginning of the war. One had a head full of red hair, while the other had dark, curly hair.

Baldric motioned for his men to halt as he approached them. The Shagin stood calmly, even facing over a dozen armed men. They were only lightly armored with padded clothing and a single sword strapped to each of their sides. Of course, it typically wasn't their weapons that were the most dangerous, but their magic.

"Where's the guardian?" the redheaded Shagin asked. Her vibrant green eyes stood out even in the darkness. Every Shagin he had seen had possessed the most stunning, jewel-colored eyes. They were an all-female race of some of the most beautiful women in the world. It was easy to see why the Immortal Warrior felt threatened by them.

"He couldn't make it," Baldric said, stepping forward and bowing in respect toward the young ladies. "I will be standing in his stead."

"He has no intention of negotiating, it seems," the dark-haired woman said, shaking her head. Her eyes were a vibrant purple color. She grabbed the other's arm. "He's wasting our time. Let's go."

"I will not be humiliated by a flunky." The redheaded Shagin brushed off the other and stepped toward Baldric, eyeing him up and down as if to see what his response would be to placate them.

"I am the King of Adgul." He extended his hand out in friendship.

"A somewhat-important flunky, it seems." The redheaded woman rolled her eyes and refused his hand.

"I have the ear of the Immortal Warrior," Baldric lied, trying to earn their trust. "He will listen to my council.

Besides, if you're so pressed for representation, where's your general?"

"I *am* the general," the redheaded Shagin sneered. She shot him a look of disgust and turned up her nose.

Baldric grimaced and rubbed the back of his head. He blushed. "I'm terribly sorry. I meant no offense. You're just so young."

"You're one to talk," she replied.

"Maybe so, but heraldry is passed through blood, not accomplishments, such as yourself." Baldric smiled.

She returned the smile. "Flattery will get you nowhere. You may call me Artemis. This is my second, Mtendere."

"It is a pleasure to meet the two of you." Baldric bowed again. "If I may, how did someone so young become the leader of the Shagin army?"

"You know little of us, it seems," Artemis said. "I am not the leader. I am simply leading the warriors here until our Champion arrives. Truth be told, it is a task I fear I am inadequate for, but as a Fury, it has fallen to me."

"You don't owe this man anything," Mtendere said. She stepped between Baldric and Artemis, poking her finger into his chest. "Why have you come here?"

"To negotiate," Baldric answered, taking a step back. To end this conflict, he would have to know when to relent. "I want to find a peaceful solution to this war."

Artemis motioned for Mtendere to stand down. "For countless generations, Shagin have been forced to live in exile from the world," Artemis said. "Those of us who have ventured out from our forest have been ostracized and killed. Your guardian has been at war with our existence for thousands of years. Is he willing to grant us our freedom? Can we rejoin the world and live in peace?"

"I..." Baldric stammered. His gaze wondered around the rocky canyon as if seeking an answer. The truth was, their hopes and dream were not a possibility under the guardian's rule. He had no options to convince her, and she knew it.

"We joined this fight to end the oppression of our sisters," Artemis said, staring into the brazier. The light of the flickering flame illuminated her face, revealing the purple bags under her eyes. "Now we face overwhelming odds and the consequences of losing will mean more suffering for our sisters and daughters. If you were us, would you surrender the chance to have your little ones live a life free of fear?"

"No, but it's worse than you think." Baldric stepped beside her. "The Immortal Warrior plans on crushing your forces. He has a plan and the resolve to carry it out. Once defeated, he will execute the leaders of each nation that have rebelled against him."

"We knew the risks the moment we joined the alliance," Artemis said. "We have no intention of losing this battle."

"Your forces have made great strides and won many battles," Baldric said. "But your lack of numbers has already betrayed you. You failed to take Valceem, and that failure has cost you your most scarce resource—time. The Immortal Warrior has gathered the armies of the Three Realms together. You are outnumbered twelve to one."

"And yet we've held you off for three days," Mtendere said, resting against the rocky wall. Her body seemed so relaxed and casual, except for her hand, which sat upon the hilt of her sword. "And nearly broke through your line yesterday."

"You bent the line, but it did not falter," Baldric reminded. "History doesn't remember the almost-had. That line has been fortified, and every day that passes weakens your forces and supplies, while his has plenty of resolve to spare."

"I'm no fool." Artemis pinched her brow. "We can't hold this valley for long. This battle—this war—has worn me down. It has worn all of us down. But how can I surrender the dreams of a better future for my sisters?"

"You'll lose if you continue to fight," Baldric said, as a matter of fact.

"We can't give in to that tyrant," Mtendere said. "Not after everything he's done. His crimes scream for justice. If anyone can lead us to victory, it is our goddess of war."

Mtendere cut her eyes toward Artemis, who blushed and covered her face. Baldric wasn't familiar with their religion. He was under the impression they only worshiped the one goddess. Or maybe that was simply a moniker Mtendere was addressing Artemis with. It could explain her rank, given her age. But by Artemis's expression, it seemed the stress of the battle was getting to her.

"This isn't about his crimes," Baldric argued, staring down at the dirt. He drew a deep breath as he raised his gaze to meet Artemis's. "This is about your survival. You've done the impossible. You've held back the weight of the world for three days. But how much more can you endure? How long until the fight runs out?"

Artemis sighed, hanging her head. "I fear you are right. This is a battle we cannot win. If Ilyia was here, maybe she could turn the tide, but my strength alone is not enough to overcome these odds for us. If I can hold out until she and the rest of the Furies arrive, maybe we'll win."

"You won't."

"Then we'll lose doing the best we can for our sisters." Artemis slammed her foot into the ground, kicking up dust and dirt. "That bastard has longed to wage war in proper against Shagin. I fear we'll cast that die the moment this battle is over. If we falter, our sisters will die, all because we chose to act and failed. As long as I draw breath, I will not allow that to happen."

"That's why I need you to negotiate with me," Baldric pleaded, shifting his weight towards her. "If we can come to terms, we can avoid further bloodshed."

Artemis faltered and looked away. "Even if we did surrender, he wouldn't just let us live. It's all we've ever wanted."

"If you lay down your arms, I will do everything in my power to prevent that from happening," Baldric said.

"And if it comes to that?" Artemis asked. Their eyes met. In the dancing light of the brazier, Baldric noticed, for the first time, the red veins running through the whites of her watery eyes.

"If it comes to that, you have my word, I will personally slay him," Baldric said, gritting his teeth together.

"Yeah, like you could," Artemis jeered. "But there's something about your sincerity I admire. I almost believe you would try."

"I am no admirer of the Immortal Warrior," Baldric clarified. "I agree with you completely. He is a tyrant and mass-murderer who slaughtered the Koroks for not believing in the right gods. I swear, one day, he will face justice, but you cannot stand against him this day. His forces are too strong, too united."

"If you truly feel this way, side with us," Artemis said, holding out her hand toward him as if she wanted him to take it. "You control one third of his forces. Join us, turn the tide of this war, and help us forge a new age."

Baldric's heart skipped. A new age. It was what Sera wanted. It was what he wanted. He swallowed hard. Part of him felt that she was right. They fought on the side of justice while he stood with cruelty. All he had to do was take a single step forward to correct that. He could move ahead.

Baldric hesitated.

"I cannot," he said.

"You're going to stand by his side after all that?" Mtendere gaze flicked up as she shook her head.

"A new age," Baldric whispered, avoiding eye contact. "I've lost everything to place myself where I am. I am in the

64

position necessary to create that new age. In his current state, I cannot stand against the Immortal Warrior without failing, and I *cannot* fail. I have a promise to keep."

"Bravado is easy," Artemis added, turning her back to Baldric. "We took the risks you're too afraid to take. You're nothing more than a coward, and you will die a coward's death."

"I swear, I will do whatever I can to lessen his wrath," Baldric said, stepping in front of her as she began to walk away. "Please."

"Empty words mean nothing." Artemis pushed past him and motioned Mtendere to follow. "All we can rely on is the strength of our resolve."

"How the hell can you expect to fight when passion is your only weapon?" Baldric screamed after her. "You will die if you fight! Tomorrow will be hell for all!"

"And failure would bring hell to my sisters." Artemis stopped and turned back toward Baldric. Her vibrant green eyes were full of fire and vigor. "We will fight for our little ones. If we die, we die."

　　* * *

The morning came, and with it—war. Baldric tried his best. Now he had little choice but to don his armor and give the atrocious order to his men, all while he waited back in safety alongside the Immortal Warrior.

Baldric stood atop the hillside as his army marched into the Shagin line, which had taken up position across the grassy plain toward the edge of the rocky canyon pass. Even at the distance, the screams of the dying pierced his ears as the two forces clashed. There was no escaping the cries of pain. Sounds bounced off the rocks that surrounded every side of the plains, echoing in the killing fields.

A Niwendian battalion was already wiped out in the first wave. Now it was his own people's turn. His jaw clenched. How could he be so powerless? Flashes of steel and magic erupted in the distance.

The day ended the same as it began, marked with the screams of the dying. The bloodiest day of the bloodiest battle was over, and without the hesitation of attempting to spare the lives of their own soldiers, the death toll doubled in a single day. At night, the coalition sent collectors onto the field to remove as many bodies as they were able, to pave the way on the field for more to fall.

The fifth day of the battle dawned and ended with another crimson bath, as did the sixth. An estimated one hundred thousand dead in six days, while the Shagin had only lost a handful. Upon the morning of the seventh day, battle began again, only this time, exhaustion slowed the Shagin response.

"Your plan appears to be working," the Immortal Warrior said to Legato. "It's taking them longer to dispatch this wave than any other. Still, this battalion is dying quicker than I hoped."

"Should we send another wave to further soften them up?" Legato asked. Baldric grimaced just hearing the words.

"That won't be necessary." The Immortal Warrior waved him off. "The line should be soft enough. We don't want too many bodies crowding the field when we engage."

"These people trusted us!" Baldric cried out.

"Steady your resolve," the Immortal Warrior said, not even bothering to face him. "In a few hours, this war will be over."

"My people are dying!"

The Immortal Warrior turned toward him and placed his hand on Baldric's shoulder and smiled. "Take it easy. They are my people, too."

Baldric's heart sank in his chest as all hope and goodness seemed to disappear from the world. Despair and pain crushed his soul.

"How can you be so callous?" Baldric said between gritted teeth. "How much more bloodshed will satisfy you?"

"I'm growing tired of your insubordination," the Immortal Warrior seethed, tightened his grip, digging his fingers into Baldric's shoulder. "Your heart is too soft. If the responsibility bothers you so much, perhaps I should find a replacement?"

Baldric tore free from the Immortal Warrior's grip. His eyes fell to the ground. If he wanted any hope of bringing about the change Sera dreamed about, he had no choice but to capitulate. "No... I'll... be fine."

"Good." He released his hold on Baldric and held out his hand, flames erupting from his palm. The flames dissipated, revealing the legendary sword, the Immortal Blade. The steel of the sword glistened and shone in shades of orange and yellow, matching the flames it appeared from. Three pairs of prongs extended out from the blade. Curving down toward the golden hilt, they resembled large arrow heads. It was this sword that the gods bestowed upon him as a symbol of his station when they gifted him an ageless life and divine fire. Or so he claimed. "It's almost our time to join the field. Take heart. We will win today and secure peace for the age."

The Immortal Warrior led the next wave into battle. He stood in front of the formation with Baldric, Legato, and Zagu directly behind, in line with the remaining troops. They marched through the dust and smoke. Bodies lay strewn across the now red grass. They had to tread carefully to step over the dead as their armored boots sank into the carmine soil.

The Shagin line was frazzled. Their faces were dirty and speckled with blood. Despite their visible exhaustion, the army of women held their ground as the Coalition forces advanced toward them. The swell of their spirit energy met Baldric, but it wasn't strength that he felt in their spirit, but desperation.

The Immortal Warrior responded in kind. His own energy erupted from him in a fiery storm as flames danced in the palm of his hands. A simple wave forward, and the flames sprung to life in a fiery vortex. The fire surrounded much of the Shagin army, and they scurried away from the edges to avoid the heat.

The Immortal Warrior smiled, and the flames grew hotter and wilder. Baldric's eyes widened as the Shagin inside the inferno grasped at their chests. He was burning up the oxygen.

Those inside tried to escape the flames, jumping through the inferno to safety, while those outside rushed to free any they could.

"Kill him!" Artemis screamed, breaking free from the ranks, and rushing toward the Immortal Warrior.

The Immortal Warrior's eyes narrowed as she charged, his stance stiffening. With a quick motion of his hand, the inferno erupted in an explosive blast, sending the Shagin warriors scattering for safety. Those who weren't quick enough were swallowed whole by the flames. Even from this distance, the blaze of the heat scorched Baldric's face, making sweat pour from his brow. He watched in horror as flesh melted from bone. The strength of the Shagin's auras provided little resistance to the divine fire of the Immortal Warrior.

As soon as the blast halted, the Immortal Warrior rushed forward while the Shagin warriors were still recovering from the chaos. He slashed and severed any in his wake. He moved with the speed and efficiency of a manslayer, killing any his blade could reach. It was like watching a dance of death and carnage.

Shagin's spirit energy provided resistance to normal attacks, but the Immortal Warrior with the Immortal Blade was anything but normal. He cleaved through meat and steel as if they were air. The Shagin were the fiercest warriors in the Three Realms. The presence of only a handful of them had been enough to secure victory in battles prior. But the Immortal Warrior had spent a thousand years honing his craft, and against his overwhelming might, their skill and magic meant nothing.

Perhaps if they were fresh, they would pose a larger threat to the guardian, but seven days of doing the impossible followed by wave upon wave of battle had dwindled their strength.

Baldric averted his eyes. The rest of the army, seeing the Immortal Warrior's fire and carnage, rushed into the fray behind him.

Zagu nudged Baldric from behind. "We must go too."

Baldric tightened his grip on his spear and moved forward into the battle. The Shagin line had scattered, as the roaring fire had broken any semblance of formation.

A Shagin warrior leapt at him as he entered the fray. He parried her attack with the tip of his spear. He rotated the shaft, bringing the point back in line and thrusted into her chest, but it did not pierce. She spun around the spear; her duel curved swords poised, ready to strike. With a single motion of one blade, she sliced his spear in half.

Baldric faltered and stumbled to his rear.

Legato leapt in front of him. He parried the warrior's attack and drove his sword through her gut. Blood erupted from her mouth, and she fell to her knees. Legato ripped his sword out, causing blood to mist in the air, splattering against Baldric's face.

"We told you these monsters use spirit energy," Legato barked. "To pierce them, you must use your own!"

Baldric wiped at the blood on his face. "I... can't."

"Sentimentality has no place on the battlefield," Legato said, hoisting Baldric to his feet. "Here you kill or be killed. Try to flee, and I will kill you myself."

"Murderous bastards!" Mtendere rushed from the chaos toward the pair. "We trusted you!"

She tossed a pair of chakrams in the air. They spun and hovered, hanging in the air above her head before launching themselves at Baldric and Legato. Baldric dove out of the way and drew his short sword.

"I don't want to fight you," he pleaded, striking a guard position as she rushed forward.

She did not stop. She leapt toward him, drawing two curved swords. She swung wildly at his head. It took everything he had to parry the dual blades. He stumbled upon the force of her blows.

"Baldric!" Legato screamed.

Baldric's eyes widened. The chakrams sprung back to life and hurtled toward him. Baldric leapt backward, dodging Mtendere's swords and spinning chakrams.

"I'll take your head if it's the last thing I do," she cried.

A liquid tentacle wrapped around his head, cutting off his air. He gasped, choking on water. Artemis's left arm had transformed into a water construct, while her right held a sword of her own.

He struggled against her pull, but the more he fought it, the tighter she held. His lungs screamed for air.

A blast of flame tore through the water, freeing Baldric. He faltered to his knees, gasping for breath. The Immortal Warrior stood facing the two leaders of the Shagin force.

"You will pay for all of my sisters killed today," Artemis said, pointing the tip of her sword at him. "We will have our freedom!"

The blade of her sword shot forward, stretching out. The Immortal Warrior parried the attack and rushed her; his own blade ready.

"I'm disappointed," he cried out, swinging the Immortal Blade. "I heard you were the best fighter the Shagin had. I guess you are all weaker than I thought."

"You bastard!" Artemis screamed, rolling out of the way of his sword. "I'll show the strength of my people!"

Baldric clenched his sword, his knuckles turning white. He had to stop this somehow. His knees buckled as he struggled to stand to his feet. How could he stop this?

"You're mine!" Mtendere cried out, her swords raised, ready to strike.

Baldric ducked, her blades missing his head by inches. Without thinking, he readied his own energy and drove his sword into her abdomen. With his own weapon spirit charged, this time the tip pierced. She let out a harrowing cry as she collapsed to the ground, blood pouring from her side.

Baldric stood over her, his sword ready to land the finishing blow. He stopped as his chest heaved from the exertion. He loosened his grip and stared into her eyes. He couldn't do this. This wasn't who he was. Now, Mtendere lay bleeding out, because of his own weakness. He dropped his sword. It fell and clanked against the blood-stained earth.

"I'm sorry," he choked. His eyes scanned the battlefield. Mounds of bodies surrounded him. Some were hacked to pieces, others incinerated. The overpowering stench of souring blood and burned flesh filled the air. The Shagin warriors had been routed and were scattering in the chaos.

Meanwhile, their leader, Artemis, desperately fought for her life against the Immortal Warrior and Legato. How could a new age be born from such chaos? What power could a king have when he sat upon a throne of blood, controlled by another?

His eyes fell. Mtendere clutched at her side, clinging to what little life she had left. His brow furrowed. It wasn't too late to make a difference, so long as he didn't give up. He'll finally do what he should have done four days ago.

"Please, I can save you."

Baldric reached out his hands toward her.

Their eyes met, and she smiled as she reached out and clasped her hands in his.

A chakram spun up beside Mtendere. It launched itself into his arms, tearing through his flesh and slicing through bone.

Baldric screamed and collapsed to the ground as blood poured from his severed arms.

"We die together!" Mtendere spat blood into his face as she tossed his severed arms beside her. She collapsed in a heap, closing her eyes.

Baldric convulsed as blood poured from his arms, and his body went into shock.

"Baldric!" the Immortal Warrior cried out. He dodged out of the way of Artemis's water arm and fired a blast of flame into her face.

"Ahh!!" Her screams pierced the air as the inferno engulfed her and spread over her entire body. She collapsed to the ground, flailing—her head and body still aflame. She swung her water arm and washed out the fire, but the damage was done. She lay screaming in the dirt, her face blackened and disfigured.

The Immortal Warrior rushed over to Baldric.

"Don't die on me," he said. He placed his hands on the stumps of Baldric's arms. His hands glowed with intense heat, searing and cauterizing the wounds shut. Baldric's eyes rolled to the back of his head as he lost consciousness.

Mtendere coughed, more blood pooling from her mouth. "I killed the man that killed us."

The Immortal Warrior sighed. He stood over Mtendere, his sword in hand. With a quick motion, he drove the blade through her skull. "Bitch."

CHAPTER FOUR

BALDRIC AWOKE SEVERAL DAYS later. The battle had long since ended. The Shagin forces fled, and it appeared the war was indeed over. The unity of the Sovereign nations had shattered. Each nations' army withdrew to defend their own borders.

In two weeks-time, the first of the Sovereign nations sued for peace, but the Triune Concordant made the law quite clear. Any nations that committed treason against the Guardian were to have its ruling class removed from power. This typically meant execution.

It seemed the Immortal Warrior knew such a drastic punishment would only cause the remaining nations to continue warring in a desperate attempt to cling to power and life. As such, he was seeking alternative solutions to deal with their uprising.

A month and a half after the Battle of Akashvani, and most of the Sovereign Nations were now discussing the terms of their surrender with the Immortal Warrior, who had proposed a solution to the ordeal.

"How can they think this?" Baldric asked, reading over the parchment given to him by Zagu. He went to rub his hand through his hair, but stopped and stared at where his arms used to be. Strange, sometimes it felt like it was still there.

"The Immortal Warrior has already agreed to these terms," Zagu said. He took the piece of parchment back before rolling it up and placing it into his coat pocket. "He requests Adgul's aid in bringing the Shagin to justice. Their elders have already agreed to surrender. Their army will lay down arms, and their leaders will turn themselves over to our custody. All we have to do is ensure peace is maintained while their leaders are executed."

"I will do no such thing!" Baldric spat. "This is ridiculous! He can't blame the entire war on the Shagin!"

"The other nations are saying they were bewitched," Zagu explained. He sighed and stroked his chin. "That is what the Shagin do after all—beguile the wills of men."

"It's an obvious lie, is what it is," Baldric said, pacing back and forth across the room. "I will not stand for this."

"That's why I'm here." Zagu motioned Baldric to stop and take a seat, but Baldric ignored him. "The Immortal Warrior recognizes your dedication and sacrifice, but you are no longer fit to rule. I am to take charge of Adgul until he crowns a new king."

"I would rather die!" Baldric stepped within inches of Zagu. His face was grim and stern.

"Look at you." Zagu grabbed hold of what was left of Baldric's left arm and held it up. "You are in no shape to resist."

Baldric pulled away and stared down at the stumps of his arms. He knew Zagu was right.

"You'll get to keep a portion of your riches and a retainer of your choice, but you will no longer be king," Zagu said sternly. He sighed. "I will send the armies to Terra one last time to aid in taking charge of the Shagin menace and controlling their lands."

Baldric's stomach sank. The new age will never come. Or maybe it was already here—an age of hatred and death. He relented and collapsed in the nearby chair.

"You took a Shagin prisoner following Akashvani." Zagu stood over him and stared down. "I understand she is a general of sorts. I'll need to know where she is imprisoned so I can extract information about their defenses."

Artemis... Baldric sighed. She had desperately clung to life and was still fighting for survival. He wouldn't allow her to be used and discarded at the guardian's whim. "She's already dead. I killed her myself."

Zagu scoffed. He paused and eyed Baldric. A sly smile fell upon his face as he placed his hand on Baldric's shoulder. "I understand. It doesn't matter. She was to be killed anyway. Just be mindful of your actions. Not even you can stand against the might of the Three Realms."

"Few can," Baldric agreed. It was all for nothing. He had lost everything—his love, his family, his kingdom, his hands—and the power to make any sort of meaningful difference. He should have joined Artemis and her people at Akashvani. The result might not have been any different, but at least he would have lost it all trying. Instead, he played the role his father had always played—the faithful servant to a tyrant.

Perhaps it wasn't too late to try. Sera wouldn't give up, and neither would he.

Baldric bid Zagu farewell and headed through Castle Drakon to find Ekene.

"My lord," Ekene said, bowing. "What news does Lord Zagu bring?"

"I'm no longer king," Baldric said, as a matter of fact. "But you are still my retainer. I need you to sneak Artemis out of the castle and toward the shipyard. I'm taking my airship, and the three of us will travel north."

"Where are we headed?" Ekene asked, a look of concern on his face.

There was still one thing he hadn't lost. The most powerful weapon in the world wasn't a sword or fire, it was knowledge. If he wanted any hope to still cling to his ideals and bring forth the new age, he would need the help of an old friend. He just hoped he could find him. "We're going to the only suitable place for a banished king, Crescentwood."

The airship reduced the travel time to Crescentwood from two months to only two days. They were able to rescue and sneak Artemis aboard. Most of her body had been severely burned and disfigured—her face taking the worst of it. They had to be careful dressing the wounds and securing them in place. Her whole body was wrapped tight in bandages to where she could barely move—not that she tried. At least she was alive.

Her spirit energy was strong, and it ensured that she survived when any other wouldn't have. Even with her strength and the best medical attention Baldric had had at his disposal, it was uncertain for how long she could go on. She barely spoke, let alone opened her eyes for more than a moment.

"Take me home," she demanded upon hearing the plans the Immortal Warrior had for her people. "I have to save them... The elders refused the war... It was us. The Furies went against the commands of the elders... We acted alone... I have to stop this... It's not right!"

"You're in no condition to fight," Baldric reminded. He stared down at his own arms. "Neither of us are. The fact is, we do not have the power to alter this course."

"You don't understand," Artemis said. Her vibrant green eyes, now bloodshot and yellowed, opened and stared into his. "I... should have... died... and now my elders will suffer in my stead... I can't let that happen... How many of my sisters will die for our mistakes?"

"I'm sorry," Baldric said, averting his gaze. "There's nothing we can do."

Artemis let out an anguished screech and tore at the bandages on her face as her body convulsed with tearless sobs. "No! I *can't*... My home..."

Baldric buried his head as tears swelled in his eyes.

From the windows of the airship, the small village tucked away in the snowy forest seemed so serene. Baldric hadn't been back here since that night. He was unsure of the welcome to expect, but at this point, what did it matter? The world was crumbling around him, and he had no alternatives left.

The airship landed just on the outskirts of the village. Baldric and Ekene disembarked and headed into the village, leaving Artemis onboard.

Baldric's heart skipped. The church lay in ruins—a reminder of his own cruelty and helplessness. The village never rebuilt it. Baldric looked around. Strange, there were no people to be found. Surely someone would have come to see the ship and the passengers it brought.

They wandered through the village; Ekene knocking on doors, but they found no one. The village had been abandoned. By the looks of it, no one had lived here in sometime. Snow had accumulated on all the structures and several roofs had caved in.

They made their way to the manor. The grand front doors had been ripped apart, the windows smashed, and debris lay strewn about. Inside, the furniture was broken and torn to pieces, curtains and drapes ripped to shreds, and any items of value that once belonged within were nowhere to be seen.

Baldric knelt next to the couch—the last place he had seen Sera. The cushions were torn open and stuffing hung out. The villagers must have looted the manor after he burned down the church.

He headed upstairs toward the library. More destruction lined the hallways and stairwells. The library door was thrown off its hinges. Inside, charred remains of books and shelving scattered around the room. Torn pages and broken glass dotted the floor. Written on the wall in red was "Devil worshippers."

Baldric dropped to his knees. There was nothing left. Nothing here would be of any use.

His foot grazed the small glass orb which once housed Sokaris. He dropped down to the floor and put his face up next to the orb, gazing into the clear glass. "I need help," Baldric whimpered, but the orb remained empty. What could he do now?

Needles pricked at the back of his mind. He stared at the orb as inky black shadows filled the glass, and a single eye opened in the swirling vortex.

"Sokaris," Baldric whispered.

"She is gone," Sokaris spoke within his mind. "You are no longer whole."

"I... failed." Baldric stared into Sokaris's unblinking eye. "I tried to change things. I tried to help bring a new age of peace and understanding, but hate was too much."

"Mortality is fleeting." Sokaris said. "Across time and space, the same cycles repeat eternally."

Baldric nodded. "Hatred and killing. So much death and blood for nothing. But what can I do against such overwhelming hate? I have no power. My kingdom has been taken from me, just like my hands. We had dreamt of the coming age, but how do I bring it about?"

"Ages don't change," Sokaris said. "Only perception."

"If nothing changes, does any of it matter?" Baldric asked. His eyes wandered around the room, fixated on the destruction. "No. But that's why our actions matter so much more."

"I have watched you through the veil," Sokaris said. "I can aid you."

"How?" Baldric asked, motioning with his severed arms.

"Your body can be restored," Sokaris said. "There is a cost."

"What is it?"

Images of inky shadows flowing into his body flooded his mind. Sokaris's power was too great to pass through the veil in his current form, but now he was showing Baldric a way around that limitation.

"A possession?" Baldric eyed Sokaris, his breath heavy and eyes wide.

"No," Sokaris said. "We would be annihilated. No more Baldric or Sokaris. A new being would form—half you. Half me."

"We would die?" Baldric's brow furrowed as he contemplated the possibility.

"Yes," Sokaris said. "Our memories would pass on, but we will cease."

"You would give up your life for me?" Baldric asked. "You're a god."

Images of Sera filled every corner of Baldric's mind. Tears swelled in his eyes and streamed down his face. He had almost forgotten how she looked. Her dark eyes haunted his thoughts. She was so vivid. The smoothness of her skin, the smile upon her face, the gentleness of her heart.

Sokaris's voice reverberated in his thoughts. "I'm discomforted at Sera's end. I understand what I wish I did not. I will rectify this. I will no longer be. I will join with you. We will bring forth a new age. The power of a god in mortal form."

Baldric nodded. His mind flashed to Artemis and her people and the many lives who perished before his very eyes. "If I can save others, my life is unimportant."

Sokaris closed his eye. "The new age begins."

Cracks formed on the orb and it shattered into pieces. The black shadows danced around Baldric, licking and flickering like flames. He closed his eyes as the inky vortex moved within him.

* * *

The Immortal Warrior leaned back in his chair as he thumbed through the pages of his journal. Doubt flooded his mind, but he pushed the thoughts out of his head. He had to be strong. His personal feelings couldn't dictate his actions. After all, it was his sentimentality that prevented him from acting against the Shagin before. If he had been stronger of will, maybe this whole war could have been avoided.

Whatever the cause, now was the time for decisive action. The only way to save the Three Realms and maintain peace and stability was to follow through with his own orders. Shifting the blame of the war off the other nations and burdening it solely on the Shagin was the only way to alleviate his own laws. Still, it made him uneasy.

They were a stubborn and proud people. That pride would have to be broken. There was no telling just what action it would take to do so.

He paused, dropping the journal to the floor as a wave of fear washed over him. His eyes widened as his heart rate quickened. What was this? He wiped at the sweat dripping down his furrowed brow as the overwhelming presence encompassed him. It was energy unlike anything he had ever felt before. It appeared so suddenly. How? Where did it come from? He jumped up from his chair.

The Aeolus Gate!

He rushed out of the chamber and through the tower's corridors toward the gate. The entrance to the chamber was open. His Torredins, the loyal knights of his tower, lay dead around the teleportation gate. His eyes scanned the corridor and stopped at the shadowy figure.

"They were hesitant to let me through," Baldric said. His face was sweaty; his hair disheveled; and his eyes, while narrow, showed a wildness he had not seen before. The Immortal Warrior stared down and fixated on Baldric's arms, whose hands were balled tight into fists.

"You shouldn't be here. This place is —"

"A tower of hate?" Baldric interrupted.

"Sacred," the Immortal Warrior responded. He took a few uneasy steps forward. Baldric didn't move. His head merely swayed side to side as if it was too heavy for his neck. "This tower belongs to the gods. I stripped you of your titles. You are no longer the Sage of Adgul. Judging from that retched aura that permeates from you, you are nothing more than a demon now."

A smile slowly crept onto Baldric's face before turning into a full-on laugh. "No, I am vengeance. I am war. I am the scorn of all those who have suffered under your heel."

"What happened to you?" The Immortal Warrior asked. There were at least a dozen of the best warriors lying dead in the chamber. The old Baldric wouldn't do such a thing—he couldn't. "Your arms grew back. What sort of devilry is this?"

"There's a fire inside of me," Baldric said, lurching forward. His body twitched as he reared up, arching his back. "Its roar tells me to destroy you!"

Baldric charged forward; his fist raised. The Immortal Warrior's eyes widened. He was fast. In a moment, he closed the distance between them. The Immortal Warrior only had time enough to jump out of the way of Baldric's strike. His fist crashed into the wall, tearing through the stone. The force of the impact erupted the wall in a shower of stone and dust.

The Immortal Warrior rolled to his feet and summoned his sword. In a blaze of fire, the Immortal Blade appeared. He stood his ground and faced his foe.

Baldric smiled and held up his right hand. His bones popped and snapped as he flexed his fingers into a fist. "I was hoping for a good fight." He rushed forward, pulling his arm back, ready to strike again. "Your tyranny ends by *my* hands!"

Baldric launched strike after strike. The Immortal Warrior leapt backward, holding his sword between the two of them and parrying each punch with the legendary steel forged by the gods themselves. The sword reverberated and groaned under the stress of each hit. Each impact sent shockwaves into his hands and threatened to rend the sword from his grasp.

The Immortal Warrior jumped backward, creating distance between the two. He stared down at his hands as blood oozed from his palms.

"What is the meaning of this?" The Immortal Warrior demanded.

"Don't you speak for the gods? How can you not know?" Baldric charged forward. The Immortal Warrior dodged and rolled out of the way of the incoming attacks, afraid to parry too many blows with his sword. "How many lives have you destroyed? All for your own ego. Just to play the guardian."

"Everything I've done," the Immortal Warrior spat back. He swung the Immortal Blade wildly at Baldric. "I've done in the name of the gods. I am their champion. They chose me!"

"Your gods are pathetic!" Baldric screamed, leaping out of the way of the slash. He crouched down and sprang up to attack again. "You hide behind myths to justify your own failures as a human being!"

The Immortal Warrior slashed with his sword. Baldric parried the blade with his bare arm, pushing it aside. He threw his other fist into The Immortal Warrior's sternum. It landed with a sick thud. The Immortal Warrior screamed out as the force of the blow lifted him off his feet and sent him hurtling across the corridor. He collapsed in a heap, coughing up blood.

"I'm going to destroy you and this tower. I will bring about the next age," Baldric said, his eyes wide. He cracked his knuckles as he strolled towards the injured guardian. "You have no place in the future I will create."

"Listen... to... me..." the Immortal Warrior said in between coughs of blood.

"I'm done listening."

The Immortal Warrior frowned. He gathered his strength, waving his hand, and fired a blast of flame at Baldric. The flames washed over the former Sage of Adgul, but left him unharmed. The Immortal Warrior gritted his teeth. He didn't even try to avoid it. This was a fight he couldn't win. Not here anyway.

He didn't wait for Baldric to respond. He took to his feet and ran out of the chamber toward the stairs.

Baldric swatted the flames away. His eyes narrowed. The Immortal Warrior couldn't escape that easily. There was nowhere he could flee to that Baldric wouldn't find him. He dug his foot into the ground and launched himself forward, springing after his foe.

Baldric bolted up the stairs and burst through the door leading out to the top of the tower. The Immortal Warrior was waiting and blasted a bolt of fire his way. Baldric dodged out of its path. His eyes narrowed as fire erupted all around the tower's top. He sprinted away from the flames as the Immortal Warrior sent blast after blast his way.

Baldric scowled. This was why he came here—more room for his flames. He scurried around the tower as the fire balls hurtled toward him. He leapt over the flames and charged toward the Immortal Warrior.

"You will die!" the Immortal Warrior cried out. He fired blast after blast of flame with one hand, while holding the Immortal Blade with the other as he attempted to keep distance between them.

"I can't die here!" Baldric charged through a wall of fire. The flames and heat licked upon his flesh. He grimaced as his flesh seared. Was his power already waning? It didn't matter. Nothing would stop him. He pressed through the flames and came within striking distance of the guardian. "Justice will prevail!"

The Immortal Warrior ducked and weaved out of Baldric's strikes. The sheer force of his punches sent shockwaves of air colliding into the Guardian's flesh. Baldric grinned. He outmatched him in strength.

"What sort of justice makes pacts with devils?" The Immortal Warrior asked through gritted teeth. "I can feel the waves of malice wafting off you."

"I'm not the one murdering their own people to fulfill their god-delusion." Baldric spun on his heel and struck the Immortal Warrior in the side of the face with a spinning heel kick.

The Immortal Warrior twirled in the air and crumbled to the ground. He rolled with the momentum back onto his feet as blood poured from his lip. "True justice can only be found in divinity. Anything that is contra to the will of heaven is evil and cannot stand."

"You cause untold suffering. How can that be just?" Baldric leapt into the air; his fist poised to strike.

The Immortal Warrior dove out of the way of Baldric's punch. The force of the impact tore away a portion of the tower's top, revealing the room below. Baldric followed the debris as he tumbled into the hole.

The Immortal Warrior readied his sword as Baldric leapt up through the roof and landed back on the tower's top.

The Immortal Warrior didn't wait for Baldric to regain his footing. He rushed forward, swinging cut after cut at Baldric, who struggled to avoid the legendary blade.

"This world is finite," The Immortal Warrior said, forcing Baldric back. "The world to come will bear the rule of the gods. Any suffering I might cause is insignificant to bring about the eternal bliss of heaven."

"That's garbage!" Baldric ducked out of the way of another slash. The blade nicked his arm, drawing blood. He had to put the Immortal Warrior back on the defensive. He had to end this fight before his power failed.

"You know it to be true," the Immortal Warrior said. His sword burst into flame as he slashed at Baldric. "We both have our own visions of the future, and will do whatever it takes to achieve that vision. Your new arms are proof of that."

"I'm not a murderer!" Baldric jumped out of the way of the flaming sword, allowing it to pass by safely. He launched himself forward and grabbed hold of the Immortal Warrior.

"What a lie!" The Immortal Warrior sent intense heat throughout his entire body. Baldric winced as the temperature of the guardian's skin burned his flesh, and he was forced to let go. "I can sense the blood on you. I can feel your hate."

The Immortal Warrior hurled a fireball at Baldric. Baldric braced for the impact. It struck him and reddened his flesh. The force of the blast sent him hurtling backwards and tumbling to the floor.

"I've not taken life out of malice!" Baldric said, forcing himself back to his feet.

"Who's delusional now? Perhaps I know more about you than you realize. We both have sacrificed to get where we are. The only difference between you and me—I bring peace and stability to the Three Realms, while you bring naivety and will threaten that stability. You believe you are some savior, while I am merely a vessel for the gods."

The Immortal Warrior raised his hand and an inferno of flame shot forward.

"A vessel for your own ego!" Baldric dove out of the way of the blast. He secured his footing as another blast hurtled toward him. He sprinted around the blast and took the Immortal Warrior's flank. "You claim to follow the will of the gods, but you only follow your own."

"I have spoken with the gods." The Immortal Warrior spun and launched another blast toward Baldric.

"And I am one!" Baldric leapt over the blast and landed on his feet.

He charged forward. The Immortal Warrior waved his hand, sending a blaze of flame toward Baldric. Baldric gritted his teeth. He ducked his head and plowed through the fire. He seized the Immortal Warrior's arm and threw him to the ground. The Immortal Warrior rolled back onto his feet.

Baldric planted his foot and launched a roundhouse kick, striking the Immortal Warrior's sword hand and sending the Immortal Blade flying away. Baldric leapt high into the air. He threw a punch downward. The Immortal Warrior dodged out of the way. Baldric slammed his fist into the stone floor, shattering the rock and sending debris and smoke into the air.

Baldric jumped forward and grabbed hold of the Immortal Warrior's throat and squeezed with all his might. The Immortal Warrior gasped and gurgled as the force crushed his windpipe. He extended his arm. A hidden dagger slid down his sleeve into his palm. With a quick motion, he stabbed Baldric in the side of the neck. The blade pierced his flesh and drove deep into his throat.

Baldric cried out, releasing his grip and stumbling backwards. The Immortal Warrior coughed and sputtered, blood oozing from his lips.

Baldric held the dagger in place and faltered to a knee.

"Go... back... to hell," the Immortal Warrior stuttered, gathering all the strength he had left. He held out both hands toward Baldric as a volcanic blast of fire erupted forth.

Baldric gasped. His weak legs failed him. The fire engulfed him. It exploded in a blaze of smoke and heat, annihilating the stone where Baldric once stood. The blast sent his inflamed body hurtling through the air and over the side of the tower careening to the earth below.

The Immortal Warrior held his throat as his strength gave way and he collapsed on top of the tower.

* * *

When the Immortal Warrior came to, he had his Torredins retrieve Baldric's body, but after hours of searching around the base of the tower, his remains were nowhere to be found.

"How is this possible?" Legato asked, leaning against the infirmary bed the Immortal Warrior laid in.

The Immortal Warrior stared at his protégé. He shook his head. "I don't know. Baldric is nothing more than a sage of evil now. Anything is possible."

"Zagu, you spoke with him last. Do you have any idea?" Legato asked, wiping the sweat from his brow.

Zagu shook his head. "I have no words." He paused as the thought donned on him. "But I might have committed treason."

"What do you mean?" the Immortal Warrior asked, sitting upright in the bed.

Zagu ducked his head in shame. "When I informed you that Baldric killed the Shagin general, I suspected he was lying at the time, but I never said."

"He's using their magic?" Legato asked, his eyes wide.

"No, it's not their magic. It's something else." The Immortal Warrior grimaced as he rubbed his injured neck. "I understand why you protected him. You've always had a soft spot for Baldric. But now the future of the Three Realms is even more at risk than it was before."

"Even if he's not using their magic, Baldric could still forge an alliance with the Shagin," Legato said. "If he does that, if he secures power in Adgul, this war will start again. Only this time, Terra will fall. Too many nations refused their alliance because they thought they would lose the war. A new alliance with Adgul and Shagin would all but guarantee victory for them."

"The Shagin no longer pose a threat," Zagu said, waving off Legato's concerns. "We are less than a day away from abolishing their military and removing their leaders."

"They are all dangerous." Legato scowled.

"What are you suggesting?" The Immortal Warrior asked, eying his sage.

"You tried to give them a peaceful death by cursing them to only birth females. That failed, and you allowed them to exist outside your rule, and they still spat in your face," Legato said, bending down and leaning on the bed. "Finish what you started. Destroy them."

The Immortal Warrior sighed. "I fear you are right." He made a covenant with the gods to secure and maintain peace within the Three Realms, regardless of his own personal misgivings and spiritual needs. It seems again, he was being called upon to sacrifice his own moral code for the greater good. Then again, an immoral action, when necessary, was the moral thing to do.

"Very well," he said. "Legato, go to Shagin. Take charge of our forces there. Purge the Shagin from existence. We will bring the full might of every nation within the Three Realms down upon them. Exterminate them to the last woman and child."

* * *

Zagu shut the door leading from the Immortal Warrior's chambers. He was in bad shape. Just how powerful had Baldric become? In over a thousand years, no one had ever posed a threat to the Immortal Warrior in combat. Now, the undefeated champion of the gods lay bedridden with near fatal damage to his throat and trachea.

Baldric was young and full of optimism. It seemed hard to accept he would make a deal with a devil for power. Even harder to accept, he would then try to usurp the Immortal Warrior.

Zagu sighed. Though part of him agreed with the rationale, the Guardian's actions against the Shagin were problematic to defend. Perhaps Baldric was correct to rebel.

Zagu made his way through the sprawling tower and toward his own quarters. Now, with Baldric dead, it was up to him to hold Adgul in line and prepare its new ruler, whoever that may be. Though, without Baldric's body, it was difficult to relax. No one could survive the sacred fire of the Immortal Warrior, not to mention the immense fall from the tower. It was nearly three thousand feet from its top to the ground below.

He shut the door to his quarters and turned around. His heart skipped. A figure sat in the corner of the room. He was badly burned and bloody. A knife protruded from his neck.

"Baldric?" Zagu whispered, leaning forward to get a better look. "How are you alive?"

"Baldric is gone," he replied, standing. "I am something new entirely. I am the champion of the hated—the embodiment of scorn."

"I don't understand." Zagu backed up against the door, his hand resting on the handle.

Baldric's eyes met Zagu's as he inched his way forward. "Everything's new to me. I don't know if I fully understand it." He stared down at his burnt flesh. "The power of the Diadriem flows through me—a being of spirit made flesh."

"I saw what you did," Zagu said, reaching out toward Baldric. "It terrifies me. Please, let me help you. Legato has the full ear of the Immortal Warrior. Your actions have spurred them to extreme measures. Whatever this is, you must stop."

"Even with this power, it wasn't enough." He stared at his hands. "No, it wasn't my power. It was my form. It will take time for my power to fully manifest in this body, assuming this body will ever be able to handle Sokaris's full might."

"What are you talking about? There's still time to make this right. We can use this power to bring about the age of peace you want."

Baldric nodded in agreement. "I would like that."

"But we have to do it the right way."

Baldric's eyes narrowed. "I tried the right way. Now the only way forward is to light the flame to forge the new age in power." There would be no more waiting. No more capitulating or negotiating in the quest to forge the new age. He extended his hand, palm up. "Until my body adjusts to my power, I will have to use alternative sources."

Zagu gasped. "Baldric!" He clutched at his chest as his essence was ripped out and absorbed into Baldric's hand. Zagu's eyes went vacant and his lifeless body collapsed in a heap.

Baldric ripped out the dagger from his neck. The wound sealed itself and healed instantly as the burns faded from his flesh. He stood restored. "I told you. I am Skorne."

PART III
Malum Valet

CHAPTER FIVE

ARTEMIS COLLAPSED NEXT TO the campfire. She stared into the flickering flames as they danced about and engulfed the wooden logs, charring them black and gray. The fire licked their surfaces, tearing through their hard exterior. Wood popped and crackled as smaller branches and twigs twisted and curled in the heat. The fire burned deep black channels in the larger logs as it carved its way into their hearts.

Regardless of how strong or sturdy the logs were on the outside, they were each withered away by the flames until nothing was left but ash.

The dancing light of the fire drew her unblinking gaze in the dark. There was no turning away. No avoiding the mesmerizing pull of the flames or the heat they emitted. Even in the cold winter air, the hotness of the fire burned her core.

She rubbed at the bandages that covered her scarred body as her skin itched and ached from the day's effort. White cloths wrapped tight around every inch of her body, hiding the damage and disfigurement to her skin. Only her eyes and mouth were visible under the wrapping. Not that she would want anyone to see her. Her face had been nearly melted off, and now, it was an unknown stranger whose reflection greeted her.

Whatever physical pain was inflicted upon her, it paled in comparison to the suffering of Shagin. The guardian declared them enemies of humanity and ordered their extermination. He killed them with the stroke of a pen, amending his fucking treaty with the Three Realms to codify their murder at the highest level of his inhumane laws.

The feckless coward didn't even have the strength of character to be upfront about his carnage. He sent word to the elders to surrender, or his army would march through Shagin. To keep the peace, Shagin complied with the Guardian's demands. Their army laid down their arms, and their warriors were imprisoned—deceived into believing it was only a temporary measure. He executed the elders as part of the peace treaty, but the killings didn't stop.

Artemis shut her eyes tight, finally breaking her stare from the flames. Her heart pounded in her heaving chest, which pulled against the tightness of her bindings.

Memories flooded her mind of her last moments of innocence. The Furies, leaders of the Shagin army, had gathered—uncertain of their path forward.

It had been twelve days since the emissary from Shika arrived at Sumner requesting Shagin support for when the Sovereign Alliance declared war against the guardian. He had offered Shagin a new start and freedom from persecution from the outside world. They could travel without restrictions and would no longer be hunted and killed for leaving their forest. The Elders had deliberated, but rejected their proposal, and so the Furies met in secret.

Mtendere jumped up from her seat, slamming her hands down on the round wooden table. The vote had been split evenly, five to five, with one undeclared. "I can't believe this! You cowards!"

"Calm down, Mtendere." Ilyia, the Champion of Shagin and leader of the Furies, said, motioning for Mtendere to retake her chair. Ilyia was beautiful and powerful with long, flowing blonde hair. Any room she walked into, she owned. Her sapphire eyes were bright and bold. She had a way of seeing all sides to a debate, yet determination enough to sway any to her will. Artemis would have followed her anywhere. "We all agreed we would not proceed unless every one of us consented."

"The risk... tis simply too great," Chaska added. Her poised and calm demeanor was in stark contrast to Mtendere's fiery outburst. She held her head high with her dark hair, amethyst-colored eyes, and red facial tattoo in the shape of two arrows. Chaska had always been overly cautious. "I must think of my little one."

"We'll *never* have another opportunity like this," Mtendere said, tapping her finger against the table in cadence with each word. Her voice was loud and resolute.

"It is meaningless to discuss this further," the gold eyed Xiao Rong said, clasping her hands in front of her. "We cannot go against the decree of the Elders."

"The Elders are not infallible." Ilyia held out her hands, palm out as she pleaded her case. "They are matriarchs, and we should heed their council but not be beholden to their fear."

"We have one matriarch on this council," Mtendere reminded, cutting her eyes toward Chaska.

"And I disagree with this action." Chaska folded her arms in front of her chest. "For the safety of our children, we cannot go to war."

Ilyia turned to Artemis. Artemis would forever remember that piercing look. The gaze of her blue eyes filled her with courage and determination. "You did not cast a vote, and you've been quiet this whole time. What do you think?"

"I'm just taking it all in." Artemis smiled as Ilyia's gaze steeled her resolve. Her heartbeat quickened. She could no longer sit and listen. It was time for her to lead. She sighed and rubbed her hand through her red hair. "Do we do nothing? Or do we rebel and go to war? It's not a decision to be made without first considering the consequences of both.

"Chaska, I understand your hesitation. You fear what will happen to your daughter if we act. But what will happen if we don't? We are condemned to a life of seclusion. You were able to pass and venture out, even if you did have to hide behind a glamour. Others are not so lucky."

The unusual eye color of her and so many others prevented them from going on Pilgrimage as they would quickly be discovered without some method of hiding their eyes.

Even those with typical colors had to be careful due to the jewel tones and vibrance of their eye colors.

Some chose to hide their eyes behind a glamour, but they didn't always take and tended to have a high fail rate.

"I have long dreamt of a day when our children would not be hated," Artemis continued, looking around the table at each of her sisters. "Now the Fates have opened a path to that day, but it is up to us to choose to take it."

"Tis merely academic," Chaska said, waving her hand as if to brush off the idea. "The Guardian's numbers are too great. They cannot be overcome."

"Maybe," Ilyia agreed, a sly grin spread across her face. "But we don't have to. If we capture Justia, his forces won't be able to move against us for some time. All we must do at that point is take control of the continent. As our influence grows, other nations will join the Alliance. We can secure the coasts and prevent his forces from landing. The fight you fear will never come."

"That seems easier said than done," Aura said, her brow furrowed. Her light blue topaz eyes and bright pink dyed hair matched her gentle spirit.

"We can do it," Ilyia said. "Numbers is all he boasts. Every one of us in this room is greater than ten of his battalions, and I, for one, will never give up."

"What if we fail?" Xiao Rong asked.

"We won't!" Mtendere slammed her fist down on the table. The impact rattled and shook its wooden frame and reverberated within the stone walls of the chamber.

"We'll only take half of our warriors with us," Ilyia added, talking with her hands. "The other half will stay to defend our home."

"The Immortal Warrior massacred the Koroks, and he has tried to slaughter us before." Chaska raised an eyebrow and stared intently at their leader. "Do you really believe he won't try to murder us again?"

The room grew quiet.

Artemis averted her gaze, staring down at her hands. It wouldn't come to that. So long as she drew breath, she would fight. They would win. The goddess was with them. She just had to convince the others to steady their morale. "Yes. And if the worst happens and we do fail, we alone will take the blame."

"How can you be so sure?" Chaska tilted her head to the side.

"The Fates would not open a path to our demise." Artemis stood from her chair and paced back and forth across the room. She stood tall and confident, just as Ilyia always had. "I keep thinking what I would be most ashamed of doing ten or twenty years from now—fighting for my sisters, for our little ones to have the opportunity to live in a world where they won't be ostracized and killed for the crime of existing or letting the only ray of hope in a thousand years fade away while I did nothing.

"Chaska, I know you fear for your daughter, but do this for her. Give her a chance to live a happy life. This is a heavy burden we will shoulder, but we will see it through to the end, and we will succeed."

Chaska pinched her brow. Her eyes flashed toward Artemis. "Let us vote again."

Artemis clenched her bandaged fist as she stared into the campfire.

It wasn't right.

It should have been her and the rest of the Furies. They acted. They moved against the will of the elders. It was selfish and arrogant of them to reject the decision of the elders, even if their cause was just. All they wanted was a better tomorrow for Shagin. It was all for nothing—no... nothing would have been a blessing.

Her lips quivered, and she opened her eyes. All Artemis could do now was stare into the flames.

Tap. Tap. Tap.

Artemis jumped at the touch on her shoulder. She jerked back wildly and clutched her fists to her chest. The teenage girl standing next to her recoiled her hand and stared with her garnet eyes wide and mouth agape.

"I didn't mean to scare you." Gayatri stepped back, but leaned forward toward Artemis. "I was calling your name, but you never responded."

Artemis rubbed her eyes and shook her head. The roughness of her bandages scratched the dry, exposed skin around her eyes. "Sorry."

The young girl squatted down beside her. "I just wanted to thank you again for saving us."

Artemis nodded and looked away. She clasped her hands together, her fingers fiddling and rubbing against each other.

"I understand," Gayatri said, eyeing her bandages. "You've been through a lot. We all have." She reached out toward Artemis, who recoiled. Gayatri stopped and her hand fell to her side. She smiled. "How did you manage to find us?"

Artemis stared over at Skorne, but remained silent. How could she explain him and his powers? She had only been around Baldric for a short time, and even then, she would hesitate to say she knew him. However, this new version—Skorne—she *definitely* did not know. His behavior—even his power—was odd.

Shagin could typically sense the spirit energy of others using their powers who were nearby, but Skorne could do far more. He could sense life energy and pinpoint the location of the source with little effort. Distance didn't even seem a factor.

Gayatri's gaze bounced back and forth between Artemis and Skorne, who stared intently into the dark jungle. "What's he doing?"

Artemis clenched her jaw. "If the goddess is still on our side, finding more of our sisters to save."

"He can do that? But Shagin is so far away!"

Artemis shrugged. "I wouldn't believe it possible, if he hadn't already done it."

Gayatri sighed. "Well, whatever the case, I'm just happy you saved us."

They weren't the first group Skorne had found, even so, it didn't feel like enough. They had set up a network of routes and safe houses to move any Shagin survivors to Gaur—a tiny seafaring town in the neighboring nation of Passonia. They had made four trips into Shagin, and each time cut deeper.

Seeing the mutilated remains of her people inflicted more pain on her than any wounds she received from the guardian.

Artemis clenched her eyes shut. "I'm sorry," she whispered. "We should have been there sooner." Her lip quivered. She swallowed hard, pushing her grief down. "I should have been there, not off licking my wounds."

"Be glad you weren't home." Gayatri stared off into the dark. "I don't think I'll ever get the sights out of my mind. Mounds of bodies and terror. It seemed like the end of the world."

"If I had known, I would have come," Artemis said, hanging her head. Just looking at the young girl—whose life should have been filled with innocence—pierced her heart. Skorne promised to help, but in the early days of the Purge, they still believed it was only an occupation, and as such, Skorne had focused on securing his power in Adgul. "We didn't know the true extent until it was too late."

Twelve weeks was all it took to murder her people.

The bulk of the guardian's army had already withdrawn, with only a token force remaining. Still, he claimed their lands as his own, and was busy dividing the ruined cities amongst his loyal servants.

"What will happen to us now?" Gayatri asked, scooting closer to Artemis, who angled her body away. "Will we be traveling to Mystikos? I've heard rumors that others had escaped and were heading there."

"Once we've saved all that can be, we'll secure ships and send you there."

It was on the sacred island of Mystikos that Shagin, when they came of age, underwent a Trial of self-reflection and discovery. The island was known only to them, so even if others hadn't escaped, there were bound to be Shagin there—little ones who only recently found their names.

Artemis turned toward Gayatri, but avoided eye contact. "Do not mention this to anyone. The future of our people rests on secrecy. No one can know about Mystikos. The world must believe we are all dead, or they will hunt you."

"It sounds like you don't plan on coming with us."

Artemis turned her head.

Gayatri reached out toward her, but recalled her hand. "I see."

"You should go be with your mother." Artemis folded her arms across her chest and leaned away from the girl. "Hold on to those you love."

Gayatri nodded. Without warning, she launched herself forward and wrapped her arms around Artemis, hugging her tight. Artemis's eyes widened. "I will."

Gayatri left the campsite and returned to the other survivors, leaving Artemis alone with the fire. What was more painful, seeing the dead or seeing the living?

She clenched her fists. The bandages on her hands tightened and dug into her charred flesh.

Everything she had known and loved was gone, all because she was too weak to stop that fucker. The fight with the guardian looped in her mind. There had to have been something she could have done differently to kill the bastard—a dodge here or a strike there. She had promised to protect her home until her last breath.

She *should* have done so.

"I find your sorrow distracting," Skorne said, from the far side of the camp. She cut her eyes toward him. He didn't even bother to turn to face her. He simply stared off into the darkness of the night. "We saved lives today. There should be no sorrow in that."

Artemis's eyes fell and fixated on the dirt and rocks surrounding the crackling fire. It didn't feel right to say she saved lives when so many were murdered because of her.

Artemis scoffed and hung her head.

They had only just returned to Gaur to resupply and escort a small group of Shagin to safety. Goddess, please let Skorne find more of her sisters hiding. The moment he found them; Artemis would set off without hesitation.

While the soldiers were busy preparing their meals, Skorne peered through the darkness, while Artemis sat alone by the fire. She found that food simply did not taste anymore. She ate occasionally, but most nights, she lacked an appetite. Skorne, on the other hand, never ate. It was unclear how he sustained himself, but whatever power he possessed was all he needed.

The captain of Skorne's elite task force dropped his pack down next to her campfire and went to work, setting a pot over the flame. Artemis crossed her arms and shifted her weight away from him. Even with that, she couldn't avoid the flames. She turned her head to see the orange and yellow dance of the fire.

"You eyin' my meal?" the captain said. Artemis gave a slight shake of her head but didn't say anything in response. "If you want some, you'll have to go catch your own."

Artemis's brow furrowed. For all their efforts, they had only managed to save eighty-seven of her sisters. A paltry number compared to over half a million people murdered.

Unfortunately, time was against them. They weren't the only ones searching, either. Small groups of the guardian's Torredins roamed the jungle as well.

"Lord Baldric," the mayor of Gaur said, approaching the campsite from behind. He rushed past Artemis and the captain and up to Skorne, but Skorne never turned in acknowledgement. Artemis stood and approached the pair to better hear what was so urgent. The mayor brandished a piece of parchment around. "We received a correspondence from the guardian. He's doubling the bounty of any Shagin found. You must leave. I'm afraid word will get out of what you've been doing here. When that happens, who knows what will become of us. The risk of helping you is too great."

Artemis glared at the mayor—another coward in a world overrun with them. After the horrors inflicted on her sisters, everyone should be willing to do anything to save the few that remained.

Fuck!

The moment word got out of what was happening to Shagin, the world should have come to their aid. They should have saved them. She should have...

Artemis's heart skipped. She was the worst of them all.

"Fear is your guiding force." Skorne didn't even turn to face the mayor. He kept staring off into the night. "All you value is money. Spread the word to all who know of our actions. Remain silent, and I will pay triple what the Immortal Warrior promised."

Artemis smiled. At least there was one person in the Three Realms not driven by their own selfish desires.

Skorne whipped around in a fury, nearly knocking the mayor over. "What are you doing!?" he screamed, a look of unbridled rage upon his face. He darted over to his captain and seized the man's arm, pulling him away from the boiling pot.

Artemis hobbled over to the pair, her knees aching and sore. She stared down at the squirming lobster with its claws tied shut, which was held tight in the captain's hand.

"I'm just cooking my dinner," the captain stammered, trying to pull away but unable to break free from Skorne's grasp. "Did... did you want some?"

"Do you have any idea what you are about to do?" Skorne tightened his grip on the man's arm, and the captain winced in pain.

"Do... do you know a good recipe?"

Skorne scowled.

Artemis reached out and put her hand on his forearm. "It's okay," she whispered. Her sapphire eyes stared into his brown. He sighed and relaxed his grip.

"Is it? That poor being is beyond terrified." Skorne reached out and slowly took the lobster from the captain. "He feels the temperature of the air and knows what fate awaits him. I sense his terror, but he knows there is no escape from what is to come. You should empathize."

Artemis clenched her jaw and stared down at the ground.

"What do you want me to do?" the captain asked. "Not eat?"

"Doing so requires you to murder others you deem lesser than yourself. You feed your hunger with their blood. How can this be acceptable?"

"That's easy to say when you don't have to eat," Artemis reminded, ignoring the fact she hadn't eaten today. "But for the rest of us, what choice do we have?"

Skorne sneered.

"How can you hold the life of that thing in such high esteem?" the captain asked, pointing to the lobster. "You've killed people. We've seen you, so don't act so righteous."

"I don't kill for my own benefit," Skorne said, staring down at the captain. "I've only killed those whose actions mandated it. Those who cause others to suffer."

"Unfortunately," Artemis said, taking hold of the lobster and slowly prying it from Skorne's hands. "We are physical beings who must eat to live. If we don't, *we* will suffer." She held up the lobster and patted his head with her wrapped fingers. "What if we minimized his suffering beforehand?"

"If you must." Skorne sighed and placed his hand above the lobster. Red waves of energy wafted up from the animal as Skorne absorbed his life force. The crustacean's tiny body went limp as he died. "Quick and near painless."

"Thank you." Artemis gave a weak smile and handed the lobster back to the captain, who tossed it into the boiling water. Its hard carapace dinged against the sides of the metal pot.

Hissing steam emitted from the lobster's shell. Skorne covered his face with his hands and kneeled next to the fire.

"Are you alright?" Artemis asked, sitting next to him. She placed a hand on his shoulder and gazed at the strange man she had come to respect.

Skorne shook his head as he slid his hands down his face. "When I close my eyes, I can feel every living being on this planet. I know when they are suffering. Every person, every animal, every insect. Hell, even the trees and grass recognize when they are harmed, as do I."

"That's a heavy burden to bear." Artemis draped her arm around him and pulled him tight to her.

"It was a burden Sokaris managed," Skorne said, pulling away from her embrace. She frowned and looked away. He didn't seem to notice. "Despite his knowledge, he didn't understand the suffering of mortal beings, and was mostly indifferent to it. Baldric, on the other hand, was far too sensitive to the suffering of others. While being Baldric has been beneficial, I fear these incompatible traits I've inherited will drive me mad."

"Perhaps the only way to avoid that is to minimize the suffering of others as you did with the lobster."

"You might be right." He turned and faced her. His gaze looked right through her, for there was nothing left to see.

Without a word, he held out his hand and poured his own energy into her, accelerating her healing and restoring her stamina. It was his energy which had carried her through her recovery. Without it, she would never have been able to keep up with his pace.

Skorne was fast and strong. Even in her prime, she would have struggled to keep up with him. Now, with her injuries, it was nearly impossible. He seemed annoyed that he had to slow himself so that she could keep up, though he never said so.

Her arms hung heavy at her side. How could her best pass so soon? She was only twenty-five years old, but her prime was already over. It didn't seem fair.

She covered her mouth and looked away. It was what she deserved. It was her decisions—her failures—which caused so much suffering. Her survival in her weakened condition was punishment dished out by the Fates. She pursed her lips together.

She deserved so much worse.

Skorne stood and turned away from the fire and stared back into the darkness. "Tomorrow, the two of us will head back into Shagin. I know where the last of them are, and we *will* save them. But more importantly, the Immortal Warrior has just arrived. Justice is at hand."

CHAPTER SIX

THE IMMORTAL WARRIOR DROVE his blade into the chest of the Shagin woman. He and his hunters had tracked down a small group hiding in the jungle. They put up a decent fight, but their defenses were nothing.

His eyes shot upward as blood sprayed against the green foliage where a hunter had been felled. The Shagin crouched low and poised like a wildcat in front of the large, lush shrubbery of the forest. Two other hunters surrounded her, but she looked hellbent on fighting to the last.

"Wait!" he called out, stopping his Torredins. He swung the Immortal Blade in an arc, slinging the blood off the sword. "You must be talented to kill one of mine. But I assure you, what you did to him, I will unleash on you tenfold."

"Goddess, give me strength," she whispered, gripping her small curved sword tight. She held the blade out with her arms fully extended, the tip pointed at the Immortal Warrior.

He squinted his eyes and rushed forward. With a single motion, his blade struck her neck and lobbed off her head.

Her body crumbled to the ground as blood pooled from her body.

He shook his head as he cleaned the blood from his steel. She wasn't talented, just determined. His head turned toward the nearby foliage. His eyes narrowed as hushed sobs emitted behind the wide, green leaves.

"Let's see what was worth killing for." The Immortal Warrior grabbed at the plant, ripping leaves and stems off. A small toddler scurried out from the foliage before falling to her rear. Her whole body trembled as she blinked her brilliant sapphire eyes and stared up at him. He held up his sword. Fear gripped the child, and she sat motionless and silent, her lips quivering as she awaited her death.

It was his own law that demanded that *all* Shagin be killed. If even one survived, their numbers could return and the stability of the Three Realms would be threatened again. He couldn't allow that to happen. He raised his sword, readying the point to drive into her tiny body.

* * *

Artemis collapsed to the jungle floor, gasping for breath. Her whole body throbbed from the exertion of the sprint through the thick foliage. Skorne had sensed the carnage from a distance, and they hurried as fast as they could, but they were too slow.

She was too slow.

She stared at the bodies of her slain sisters that lay strewn across the ground. Blood stained the lush green landscape red, still warm from the recent massacre. She dropped to her knees and covered her face. Her heart couldn't take anymore.

It was a sight she was becoming all too familiar with. Mounds of bodies dotted their forest. The Torredin bastards didn't even have the decency to bury the dead in mass graves. Instead, they were piled high in ditches, thrown in the rivers, or left where they fell.

While Shagin's warriors were known for their magic and veracity, most of the people were just like any other. They lived their lives as bakers and farmers and school teachers. Without an army to defend themselves, they stood little hope against the *millions* the bastard guardian marched through Nebura's Pass and into their forest.

Such an overwhelming force, armed against so few.

"It's my fault," she whimpered, banging her fists in the dirt. "Everyone's dead."

Skorne placed his hand on her shoulder, and she raised her head and looked up at him.

"No." He pointed to a large tree nearby. Long ropey vines dripped off the tree and curled around its trunk. "Someone ran into that tree and disappeared. They may still be alive or they may not, but I cannot sense them."

Artemis squinted. "The tree?" Her eyes widened as a wide grin spread across her face. She jumped up and ran to it, placing her hand on the bark. "Of course!"

She gathered her spirit energy and sent it flowing into the wood. Without another word, she phased into the tree and disappeared.

Gone was the forest. Instead, she phased through a wooden door into a tiny cabin. A woman huddled in the corner stared up at her as she stepped further into the cottage. The woman's emerald eyes were wet and red from crying.

"It's okay, now," Artemis reassured her, holding up her hands as she inched toward her. "I'm one of your sisters. We can take you to safety."

"The others?" the woman asked, her voice cracking.

Artemis stopped her approach. She gritted her teeth and shook her head.

The woman closed her eyes as tears poured down her face. Artemis kneeled beside her and wrapped her arms around the woman.

"You did the right thing." Artemis understood what the proper things to say in a situation such as this, but the words felt hollow in her own ears. "You survived."

"We set this up as a last resort," the woman explained, motioning to the cabin they were in. "We were trying to escape. I ran when I saw them."

"It's going to be alright," Artemis lied, avoiding eye contact. Nothing would ever be okay. "What's your name?"

"Da-eun daughter of Ae-cha."

"Well, Da-eun, I'm..." Artemis trailed off, her gaze falling to the ground. "Lydia. Let's get you out of here."

Artemis helped Da-eun up and out through the door. They phased through the tree, back into the Latari Forest. Bright snatches of sun peered through the jungle's canopy, welcoming them back to the lush green, stained red with the blood of their sisters.

Skorne tilted his head as they appeared.

"It's a hiding tree." Artemis smiled, helping Da-eun cross the threshold. It was impressive they were able to fasten it so quickly. Whoever did it must have been a skilled enchanter. "They created a doorway to a pocket dimension. That's why you couldn't sense her when she passed through."

"Clever," Skorne said, his gaze narrowing.

"By the goddess," Da-eun whimpered. She faltered to her knees as she stared at the dead. "No, no, no, no, no."

"It's not your fault." Artemis rolled her eyes and looked away. Da-eun appeared to be no warrior. It was a warrior's duty to fight to the end—to lay down her life for her sisters—Artemis reminded herself, swallowing down the lump forming in her throat. Da-eun would bear no such responsibility. "They would have killed you, too."

"My sister..." she murmured, placing a hand on a decapitated woman. Da-eun's head sprung up as she frantically looked around the forest. "My niece! Where's my niece?"

"The child." Skorne surmised, stroking his chin. "I felt the Immortal Warrior take her. I don't know why, but she lives."

"Who are you?" Da-eun approached Skorne, eyeing him with a look of concern.

"This is King Baldric of Adgul," Artemis said, leaning against a nearby tree for support. Her shoulders bowed forward. She was more tired than she realized. She stared down at the red patches that spotted her. Her white wrappings collected dirt and filth so easily, but it seemed amongst the carnage of death, the blood of her sisters soaked its way into her coverings.

It was blood spilled because of her.

Da-eun collapsed to the ground, her eyes fixated on Skorne. "A sage?" Her voice trembled. No doubt she expected all three sages aligned with the guardian.

"I will ensure the Immortal Warrior pays for his crimes." He held out his hand to Da-eun. She stared quizzically at his outstretched hand. Her eyes darted toward Artemis, who gave her a reassuring nod. Da-eun slowly reached out and took his hand, and he helped her stand to her feet. "What is your niece's name?"

"We don't name our little ones," Artemis said, staring down at the dead. "When they come of age, they undergo a Trial. It is a sacred rite of self-discovery where we choose our names based on who we are or what we hope to represent."

"That I understand." Skorne tilted his head to the side and stared at Artemis. "What does your name mean?"

"The protector of young girls."

Dread filled her heart. She didn't deserve her name. She didn't deserve her sisterhood.

Artemis sighed and grabbed a black cloth from the ruined encampment. She draped the cloth over the decapitated body and kneeled beside it.

"Goddess, guide their spirits as they return to the Fates," she prayed, bowing her head.

"Is that where your dead go?" Skorne asked, stepping beside her.

"It is." Artemis leaned her head back and stared up through the forest canopy. Patches of the blue sky shone through the green leaves. "Nebura's essence lives within each of us. She gave her life so that Shagin would live. For her bravery, the Fates allowed her to be reborn as the stars. When we die, our bodies rest, but our spirit returns to the Fates, who will use our essence to create a new star in the sky. We live on with our goddess, shining bright in the heavens, looking down upon our loved ones."

Artemis rubbed her covered face with her cloth-wrapped hand. One day, she would join her sisters.

"I'm unsure what will happen to me when I die." Skorne stared down into the unseeing eyes of a corpse. "Baldric didn't believe in an afterlife, and the Diadriem can't die. Will I turn to meat and rot like Baldric, or form a new body and be reborn like Sokaris?"

Artemis's heart sank, hearing his words. He was wrong. Her sisters wouldn't rot. They couldn't. Their bodies might fade away, but their spirits lived on. They *had* to.

"Mortality is so stupid." Skorne pinched his brow. "Your lives are so short and fragile and full of pointless cruelty and suffering. I could have stopped this if my power was at its fullest. I was arrogant when I faced the Immortal Warrior last. Thinking myself a god. First it was my powerlessness, then my hubris, and now my ignorance." Skorne's eyes met Da-eun's. "Gather your strength and come with me. We're ending this now."

 * * *

"Where have you been?" Legato asked, rushing into the Immortal Warrior's quarters.

"Sorry, I had... preparations to make." The Immortal Warrior sighed and stood from his desk. He gently closed his journal and tossed a pen down next to it on the desk. "I'm sure by now you feel it, too. That ungodly power racing towards us."

"It feels... wrong," Legato said, frowning. It had been that presence which sent him into a spiral. The moment he sensed it, he sought the Immortal Warrior's guidance, but he was nowhere to be found. The sentries stationed at the Aeolus Gate mentioned he traveled away from their base through the portal. At least he was back now. Whatever that power was, it dwarfed his own might. "What is it?"

"That is the Sage of Evil." The Immortal Warrior circled around his desk, stopping in front of Legato. His face solemn. "Baldric has found me."

"We should kill this monster and be done with it," Legato said. How could that upstart betray them like this?

"If it was as simple as that, I would have done it." The Immortal Warrior scoffed and placed a reassuring hand on Legato's shoulder. "Baldric had referred to the devil that possessed him with the name Sokaris. Are you familiar with this name?"

Legato shook his head.

"It is one of the Diadriem, a demon god from the bowels of hell. Shortly after the gods formed our world, the Diadriem took physical forms. Out of jealousy, they created the demon world and all the forces of hell to challenge the gods. Sokaris the Soul Stealer was the worst of these devils. Our only saving grace was the barriers between worlds the gods created to protect us."

"If Baldric is truly possessed by this Sokaris, how do we stop such a thing?"

The Immortal Warrior shook his head as he headed back to the desk and picked up his journal. "Baldric died the moment he allowed the devil to pass into him. In a physical confrontation, I don't know if we can win. Our only hope is to pray there is some part of Baldric's soul left in the beast's belly."

"You intend to reason with him?"

"We maintain stability using every tool available." The Immortal Warrior held his journal up toward Legato's face. "We have no other answer to his overwhelming power."

"I... understand." Legato hung his head. Was Baldric really that powerful? He had never seen the Immortal Warrior so pessimistic. The gods blessed the Immortal Warrior. He carried their favor, and that had always been enough. It was impossible to think a devil could threaten the champion of the gods. Legato pushed the thought out of his mind. "We'll see this through."

"No. Just me." He handed the book to Legato, nearly shoving it into his hands. "Take my journal and return to the tower. I've written instructions for you within. You must ready our forces to defeat this evil by any means necessary."

"You... you don't intend to come back," Legato surmised.

"I'm counting on you to take care of everyone." The Immortal Warrior turned toward the door. "Once you've passed through the Aeolus Gate, have the guards dismantle it. If I can't stop this devil, every minute will be precious."

* * *

Artemis, Skorne, and Da-eun arrived at the coastal village of Sippar. The Guardian had fortified the once small village and turned it into a naval base. Skorne had no intentions of relying on subterfuge. He led the trio through the forest, straight toward the village gate.

A bell rang out from the watchtower, and it wasn't long before soldiers poured out of the encampment with their weapons drawn, ready to face them.

Artemis gathered her energy. She hadn't fought since Akashvani, as Skorne had fought for the both of them. She wasn't even sure she could still use her powers to their full extent, but it was clear Da-eun was no fighter. Skorne could handle the bulk of the enemy, but she would need to protect Da-eun when chaos erupted.

Skorne held up his hand toward the Guardian's forces as they gathered in formation to protect the gate. The swell of his energy sent ripples down Artemis's spine. She dug her heels into the dirt. These were soldiers of death and chaos.

They had slaughtered thousands of innocents and showed no mercy. Now they would receive none.

"Halt!" the Immortal Warrior cried out as he ran through the formation and out to meet them. "Sokaris! I am willing to negotiate."

"Negotiate!?" Artemis screamed. She lunged forward. Skorne held out his hand and stopped her. Her heart burned with fury at the fucker's audacity. "You murdered us!"

Skorne placed a hand on Artemis's shoulder and gave her a knowing wink.

Her eyes narrowed, and her mouth hung open, agape. Did he just wink?

She shook the thought from her mind. It didn't matter. She closed her eyes, taking a deep breath. The guardian would get what he deserved, and then she would piss on his grave.

"It's Skorne, by the way," he said, rolling his eyes. "She's brash, but has a point. You commit genocide and when death comes for you, you cower?"

"What is it you want?" the Immortal Warrior demanded, standing his ground.

Artemis's eyes narrowed, and a sly grin creeped across her face. She wanted him to resist. She wanted him to summon his fucking sword, just so she could watch Skorne break it in half before he did the same to him.

"My niece." Da-eun stepped forward, her voice cracking. Artemis's heart skipped, her smile faded, and her gaze fell. She had almost forgotten. "Where is she?"

"The girl?" The Immortal Warrior's brow furrowed. "All this over a babe?"

"She's not far from here." Skorne pointed in the direction he felt her life force. "To the east."

"I won't let you take her from here," the Immortal Warrior said, positioning himself directly in between them and the gate.

"Just give her back!" Da-eun screamed

"You can't keep her from me," Skorne said as a matter of fact.

"When I saw Rachel, I spared her out of pity."

"You named her!?" Artemis balled her fists tight. "You fucking bastard!"

"What can a dying culture give her?" the Immortal Warrior asked. "We can provide a better life for her than any of you ever could. She will grow in a life of luxury, and no one will ever know her origins. If she goes with you, she'll be hunted for the rest of her life."

"By you, you fucking monster," Artemis snarled. He was a heartless bastard. The old her would impale him through his black heart. She clenched her jaw. Now, she how to rely on others to fight for her.

The Immortal Warrior cut his eyes toward her. "I see you've survived my flames. That can be remedied."

"You won't get the chance," Skorne said, stepping forward. "We are taking the child and your life. You will pay for the atrocities you've committed, and we will forge a new age with your blood."

"A forge shapes through fire." The Immortal Warrior assumed a fighting stance as spinning flames swirled around him. Skorne's eyes twitched.

Artemis's chest tightened as she stepped backward. She wrapped her arms around herself, tucking her hands into her armpits as the flames sent a wave of chill washing over her. She blinked as the swirling flames encircled the guardian. She couldn't do this. Not again...

Her eyes darted back into the forest—back to safety.

"Are you okay?" Da-eun asked.

Artemis stared into the young woman's eyes.

She wasn't okay, but that no longer mattered. No more of their little ones were going to suffer and die due to her actions. She nodded and forced her foot forward, taking a single step toward the flames.

The Immortal Warrior reached toward Skorne. "Baldric, if there is any humanity left in you, please listen to me."

"Humanity?" Skorne cocked his head to the side. "Is this what humanity is? You inflict atrocities on each other for petty differences or to feed your own greed. If that is humanity, I want no part." He raised his arm, pointing his palm at the formation of soldiers in front of the village gate. "The two of you go and rescue your family. I'll cut you a path."

Green energy swirled around his hand. In a brilliant flash of green, a beam of energy erupted from his palm, roaring like thunder. The beam tore through the air, obliterating everything in its path. The shockwave from the blast ripped apart the ground, tearing out a large trench running the path of the beam. Buildings, people, foliage—anything in the beam's path disintegrated in an instant.

The Immortal Warrior stood trembling before the power unleashed. The formation of soldiers, the gate, and much of the village were gone.

Artemis couldn't stand and bask in the immense display of power, nor did she wait for the guardian to respond. She grabbed Da-eun's hand and pulled her with her as she darted into the opening Skorne created.

"We have to move!" She sprinted into the village, half dragging Da-eun behind her. Her eyes darted back for a moment as Skorne squared off with the Immortal Warrior. "Kill him."

They ran through the smoldering trench and into the village. How were they going to find her? Hopefully, Skorne's aim with that blast was accurate.

The remains of the village were filled with people fleeing from the buildings and running away to safety. It's what they deserved for stealing their homes.

Two soldiers ran through the sparse crowd with swords drawn as they charged toward them. Artemis gritted her teeth. She could do this. She could still fight. She gathered her energy, charging it through her body.

"Get behind me!"

Artemis pushed Da-eun back and stood facing the soldiers. She focused her power into her arms. With a single swing, her arm liquified, turning into water. The strain sent shockwaves of pain pulsating through her body. She grimaced, but couldn't afford to yield to the pain.

She swung her water arm, striking the first soldier. The force of the blow lifted him off his feet and sent him careening into a nearby wall, knocking him unconscious.

"You bitch!" the other soldier screamed, charging forward.

Artemis dug her heels into the dirt and swung her arm toward him.

"Ahh!" she screamed as searing pain flooded her body. Her arm reverted to normal, and she collapsed on all fours. Damn it...

The soldier rushed forward and thrust his blade at her. Her eyes widened. She rolled out of the way of the point and spun on the ground, sweeping his legs out from under him

He grunted as he hit the ground. Artemis latched onto him, wrestling him away from his weapon. He fought against her, trying to get back to his feet, but she held tight, grappling, and manipulating his body on the ground.

"Damn it! Hold still!" She transitioned her way to a back mount and wrapped her legs around his midsection and an arm around his neck. Her other hand drew the dagger he had strapped to his side. Before he could break free, she pressed the blade against the flesh of his throat.

"You motherfuckers took a child from us," Artemis said through gritted teeth. Her chest heaved as she struggled to catch her breath. "If you want to live, tell me where she is."

"I'm not sure." The soldier gasped as he tried to break free from her grip.

"Doesn't sound like he values his life," Da-eun said, her eyes locking with Artemis's, who gave her a knowing nod.

"Wait," the soldier said as Artemis pressed the dagger into his flesh, drawing blood. "I saw them take a little girl. I believe they went into that building there." He pointed to a nearby house.

"If you are lying, I'll be back for you." Artemis released her hold of the man and stood to her feet. The soldier held his bleeding neck as Artemis took off running toward the house.

"You should have killed him," Da-eun said, running behind Artemis. "It's what they would have done to us."

"I'm not them." Despite her protest, she partly agreed with Da-eun, still she had never killed an unarmed prisoner before. It was the small acts of honor and mercy which separated her from the villains who slaughtered her sisters. Though, maybe in this current world, there was no place for such naïve ideals. She supposed only time would tell.

THE ANNALS OF SKORNE

Artemis held tight to the dagger. She wasn't healed, and her powers were still too unstable to rely on. She would need the weapon if it came to a fight.

They kicked down the door and rushed into the house. A man stood behind a table. Held tightly in his arms was a small girl.

"Auntie..." Her eyes lightened as they entered, and she reached out toward Da-eun.

"What do you want?" the man asked, tightening his arms around the girl.

"My niece—give her to me." Da-eun started toward the man. Artemis reached out and halted her advance, her eyes fixated on the man's hand, which rested unnaturally near the child's neck. Da-eun halted her advance. She reached out toward the girl. "Daughter of Ga-eun, it will be okay."

"All we want is her," Artemis said, pointing the dagger at him. What could she do?

"Your niece?" the man said, his eyes bouncing back and forth between the girl and Da-eun. The daughter of Ga-eun whimpered as she looked up at the man. "I'm sorry. I cannot do that."

"I am her family!" Da-eun screamed.

"I convinced the Immortal Warrior to spare her." The man sneered, with a look of pure hatred on his face. Artemis glowered at him as her grip tightened around the dagger. "She would have been killed without my intervention. The Guardian has made it clear, if she discovers her heritage—if

I return her to your custody—her life is forfeit. I cannot doom her to the gallows."

"That bastard will be dead soon," Artemis said. She was powerless in her current state to free the child, but maybe fear could still be used as a weapon. "As will you if you don't release her."

"That's doubtful." The man bit his lip as his brow crinkled. "Even so, the Triune Concordant now specifies that all Shagin are to be executed. Others will hunt her down along with you."

Artemis clenched her jaw. This man had no sense of right. He was ready to steal a child from her family. There was no telling what else he was willing to do. She was going to need an opening. Goddess, grant her speed and strength for what was about to come.

He stepped forward, his head low. "If you want what is best for her, let me take her. I can guarantee her safety. You cannot."

"Don't you dare say that!" Da-eun screamed.

"How could you be so heartless?" Artemis clenched the dagger in her hand. Could she throw it? At one point she could have, but her body no longer always cooperated with her desires. "You don't even see us as human. You Torredin fuckers are all the same. If you value your life, cut the bullshit and release the girl."

"I promise you, Racheal will be taken care of. I have a son and two daughters. She will be happy and safe with my family." The man looked down at the daughter of Ga-eun, his hand moving away from her neck.

Now was Artemis's chance. Her hands trembled. The opening was too small. She couldn't risk it.

"I know this is difficult. But Shagin take babies to be raised in your forest all the time. I am merely taking one back. If you truly love her—if you truly want what is best for her—just walk away."

Artemis's eyes narrowed, and her blood boiled. They weren't going to solve this with words. If only her powers were more stable.

She steadied her resolve. She could do it. The pain was brief and momentary. All she had to do was land one good hit. She gritted her teeth.

No. The old her was gone. She couldn't lament that now. She had to find some way to guarantee the daughter of Ga-eun's safety. But how?

"I mean, look at you," the man said, arching his brows as a pleading look spread across his face. "You're covered in rags, and you look like death. I'm doing you a favor by taking care of her. She will be killed if she goes with you. Please don't let your selfishness create another victim."

Artemis's blood boiled over. Rage flashed through her, and she erupted with a guttural roar. Without thinking, she launched forward, leaping over the table. Her sudden action startled the man who stumbled backward, dropping the girl.

Artemis grabbed her before she could hit the ground. She kicked the man in the stomach. He hunched over and stumbled backward from the impact. She released the girl and dove at the man, tackling him to the floor.

She raised the dagger and sliced at his head, tearing through flesh and drawing blood.

"Please, no!" he cried out.

"We just wanted to live in peace." Artemis seized the man by the throat. "Why was that our crime? Our families, our children—they are all dead. And yet—why are we still here?"

Artemis's heart skipped. She was once the fiercest warrior in Shagin. She was a protector of the innocent and a fighter for freedom. Now she was scarred beyond recognition. Scars that ran deeper than flesh. They burned away her very core until she was nothing but hollow. What had they made her? What was left?

"Get the girl out of here," Artemis said, pressing the dagger firmly against the man's throat. She couldn't tell if Da-eun responded. All she could hear was the pounding in her ears and her heart pounding in her chest. "She doesn't need to see this."

* * *

"Now that I have your attention." Skorne smiled, motioning to the blast area of his attack. "Today, you fall by my hands."

"I will not let you win!" the Immortal Warrior screamed as flames swirled around him.

"Is that the best you can do?" Skorne laughed and crossed his arms. "I can barely feel your power. I fear you won't be able to provide me with a decent challenge."

"I'll show you the power of my sacred flames!" The Immortal Warrior held out both of his hands together. "Let the power of the gods burn you to ash!"

A volcanic blaze exploded from his palms. The heat of the blast ignited the nearby grass and warped the air, but Skorne did not move. The fiery inferno engulfed him.

He stood with his arms folded inside the vortex of flame as the ground beneath his feet melted from the heat. Skorne sighed. The strongest fighter in the Three Realms was no match for him. There was nothing left to do but end this charade.

Skorne walked through the fire toward the Immortal Warrior.

"Why won't you die!?" the Immortal Warrior screamed.

Skorne seized the Immortal Warrior's hands. With a single motion, he crushed both, shattering bone.

The Immortal Warrior screamed and faltered to his knees as the fire stopped.

"Perhaps you should have tried your silly sword," Skorne taunted. "At least then you might have managed to cut a few of my hairs."

"You... won't... win," the Immortal Warrior stammered.

"No," Skorne agreed, his gaze piercing through to the Immortal Warrior's soul. "I think you've already seen to that. Everyone lost!"

Skorne hurled the Immortal Warrior through the air. He slammed into the nearby watchtower. The force of the impact shattered the wooden and stone structure, demolishing it in a rain of dust and debris.

The Immortal Warrior dragged himself out from the rubble. "You must know... you will be stopped."

"What I know," Skorne said, reaching down and pulling the Immortal Warrior up from the ruins. He held him off the ground with one arm. "Is that it will not be by you."

Skorne reared back and launched a punch with all his might. His fist collided with the Immortal Warrior's chest, snapping bone, collapsing his lungs, and tearing through flesh. His fist pierced through the Immortal Warrior's body and broke free from his back in a fountain of blood.

The Immortal Warrior didn't have time to scream as shock overtook him. He convulsed as his eyes rolled to the back of his head. Skorne ripped his arm free, and the Immortal Warrior went limp and crumbled to a heap. Skorne stared down at his nemesis as blood pooled around him and the Immortal Warrior's life force faded away.

"Disappointing." Skorne cocked his head to the side as blood dripped from his arm.

He looked around at the chaos he inflicted. Smoldering ruins followed the trench of his explosive power. Many lives had vanished in an instant. Any that survived had scurried away. The watchtower lay in splinters, and at its base was the body of his enemy.

He averted his gaze from the carnage.

How very human of him.

There was no satisfaction in the Immortal Warrior's death. Vengeance did not cease the overwhelming emotions that still sprung up within him. Justice did not restore life to those he had slaughtered or heal the pain his regime had wreaked on others throughout the one thousand years of his rule.

It only lowered Skorne to his level. In his current state, if he seized control of the Three Realms, nothing could stop him from becoming the new guardian. He would become just like the Immortal Warrior, so sure of his own righteousness, he wouldn't be able to stop himself from committing the same mistakes of the past. Maybe not the exact same mistakes, but all new ones in the same vein.

How could he forge a new age when all he could do was repeat the misdeeds of the old?

It would take someone of iron resolve to shatter the chains and end the eternal cycles. Did anyone like that exist?

Skorne's eyes lit up as a wave of fear washed over him. The panicked presence was nearby.

Artemis!

He might not be the embodiment of Sera's ideals, but perhaps it wasn't too late to sow the seeds for the new age. He spun on his heels and rushed into the village.

* * *

Artemis stood over the man, her dagger pressed firmly at his throat. He deserved to die. They all did for what they've done.

Her heart jumped as the door to the house was torn off its hinges and hurtled into the street.

"What are you doing?" Skorne asked, rushing in to the house.

"Everyone's dead!" Artemis screamed, sobbing. "They killed our little ones! They all deserve to die!"

"Don't do that." Skorne inched over to her and placed his hand on her shoulder. "It's over. There's no need for more death."

"Our blood demands vengeance!" Da-eun cut her eyes toward him as she wrapped an arm around her niece and covered the girl's eyes with her free hand.

"Please…" the man begged, his whole-body trembling. "I have a family. I don't want to die."

"How many of my sisters begged for their lives?" Artemis demanded. "How many cried out for help? Help that never came."

"I can feel your conflict," Skorne said. "Put the dagger down."

"Why did I live when others died?" Artemis's face fell, but she held the knife firmly in place. "One more kill… then I'll rest."

"The pain you feel." Skorne reached a hand out toward her. "Do you really want to inflict it on others? Throughout the cosmos, the same cycles repeat, eternally so. These cycles must be broken."

"It *will* be when they are all dead," Da-eun said, her words as sharp as a razor's edge. "How can you ask us to show mercy to this scumbag? Just look at you, covered in blood. How many did you kill just moments ago?"

"I was wrong." Skorne hung his head in shame. "I am wrong. I fear I've just started the next cycle."

"Look at our dead sisters and tell me we are wrong to seek revenge," Da-eun snarled, pointing outside.

"I can't make it stop." Artemis's lips quivered as tears swelled in her eyes. "How will it ever be okay?"

"I don't know," Skorne said. "I don't know if these cycles can be broken, but someone must make the first step. Someone must try."

"Don't listen to him." Da-eun glared at Skorne, shooting daggers with her eyes. "He's not one of us. He doesn't care."

"I... I don't know if I can." Artemis's arms were so heavy. Her body was tired. Her spirit cried for rest, but it was the spirit of her people that cried for justice.

"We'll do this together." Da-eun took Artemis's hand in her own.

"Please... no," Artemis whimpered, but she put up no resistance to Da-eun's force.

The tip of the dagger pierced the man's neck. His eyes widened as tears streamed down his cheeks. Artemis closed her eyes as they drove the dagger into the man's neck. He convulsed and spasmed as blood oozed from the wound.

Skorne turned and looked away. "It *always* repeats..." He buried his face in his hands, rubbing at his skin.

"Now it's over," Da-eun said, pulling Artemis's hand backward and the dagger out of the man's neck. The wrappings around her hand were stained crimson to the point where it was hard to believe they were ever any other color.

Artemis held the dagger tight in her grip as Da-eun released her hand. It wasn't over for her. It would never be over for her. There was too much death—too much blood on her hands. She could not begin anew. She turned and pointed the dagger toward herself. "I'm so tired."

Skorne launched forward and grabbed the blade, crushing it in his hands. "Today is not your death."

"Don't I get to rest?" Artemis asked, faltering to her knees.

"You've earned one," Skorne agreed, wrapping his arms around her. "But Shagin isn't dead, and your sisters still need help. There is still a world for you to fight for."

"I don't know what kind of world it is." Artemis closed her eyes tight and leaned her head against him as warm tears streamed down her face and seeped into her bandages.

"Neither do I."

* * *

Artemis and Skorne escorted Da-eun and her niece to Gaur, where they rejoined the other Shagin survivors. Skorne purchased a ship for them to take them on their way.

Artemis sat on a rock overlooking the pier. Their work was done. Skorne couldn't feel any other survivors in Shagin. The few that they rescued would join the others on Mystikos. It would be a life of secrecy, exiled from the rest of the world, but at least they would live.

She wasn't sure where she belonged anymore. It didn't feel right to rejoin her sisters. After all, she was the reason so many of them were dead. She couldn't look any of them in the eye, knowing how great her shame and failure were.

"I thought I would find you here," Skorne said, walking up to her. "Are you not going with them?"

"No." Artemis shook her head as she wrapped her arms around herself. "I'm not worthy of being their sister anymore."

"I suspected you wouldn't go," Skorne said. "I have a confession. When I told you I couldn't find any more Shagin... I lied."

Artemis jumped up from the rock and spun toward him. Her eyes widened as tears swelled. Standing behind Skorne was Ilyia, the Champion of Shagin and leader of the Furies.

"Ilyia!" Artemis ran out and threw her arms around her Shagin sister.

"Goddess blessed us, you're alive!" A wide smile spread across Ilyia's face. She held Artemis out at arm's length. "I'm so sorry for not being there at Akashvani. It should have been me he burned."

Artemis shook her head. "Don't do that to yourself. This was the path the Fates made for us."

"How did you survive?" Ilyia embraced her again, hugging her tight.

For once in a very long time, Artemis felt whole again. For a brief moment she could pretend she was the naïve, innocent girl following her hero again.

"Luck mostly." She turned her head and smiled at Skorne. "That and Skorne. I would have died if not for him."

Ilyia faced toward Skorne and extended her hand. "Thank you for keeping her safe."

Skorne nodded and shook her hand. "Of course."

"There's more," Artemis said. This would be the best part—the look on her face upon receiving the gift of vengeance. "He killed the Immortal Warrior."

Ilyia's eyes widened and her jaw dropped. "What?"

Skorne tilted his head forward, giving his head a slight bow. "I know it's of no consolation, but we have avenged your people."

"So, there's no guardian?" Ilyia asked, sitting down on the rock as she processed the news.

"Legato Pierpont will most likely assume the title, but I don't plan on him holding it for long."

"What are we to do?" Artemis asked, taking a seat next to her leader. "Are we to join our sisters? I don't know if I can."

"I agree." Ilyia sighed and rubbed her brow. "We are warriors. Hiding from our failures does not suit us. Our home has fallen into the hands of Torredins, but the fight is only over if we allow it to be."

"What do you suggest?"

THE ANNALS OF SKORNE

"Aura, Odina, Chaska, and Ninkashi have also sur-vived." Ilyia replied.

Artemis's heart fluttered hearing the names of so many of her friends and comrades having survived the Purge. Her smile faded at all the names that weren't mentioned.

Ilyia must have sensed her sorrow as she placed her hand on top of hers. "We will reclaim our home and bring our sisters back. We can still save Shagin. That is how we will atone for our sins."

Artemis rubbed her neck. Six Furies against thousands of Torredins. A sly grin creeped upon her face. She liked those odds.

"A noble cause." Skorne licked his lips, and he held up a finger. "But I fear it will be a difficult and long task. Money, supplies, resources, whatever you need from me, you have but to ask."

"You would do that for us?" Ilyia asked, nearly falling off the rock in shock.

"Do you think I need money?" Skorne smiled. "Your people deserve justice. May the strength of your convic-tions help forge a new age."

"A new age?" Ilyia repeated. She rolled her tongue as the words reverberated in her speech. "I like the sound of that."

"Thank you." Artemis jumped up and wrapped her arms around Skorne. "For everything."

"Of course," Skorne said, bidding them farewell.

* * *

Skorne took the Aeolus Gate back to Drakon in Adgul and summoned the Rashurate, the council of the highest-ranking leaders of the realm. Skorne sat at the head of the large stone table while his council bickered amongst themselves about Adgul's next actions now that the guardian was gone.

"Thank you for your support," Skorne said, silencing the council. "You all sacrificed for our goal. While we failed to prevent genocide, we have held the Immortal Warrior accountable for his actions. With him gone, the Three Realms can finally move towards peace once again."

"We should open up negotiations with Terra right away," the Grand Vizier of the Middle Kingdom said. "The famine season is fast approaching, and with this new power, perhaps we can secure food and water from a Realm with plenty."

"Why stop there?" the Sarmeer of Ramil asked. "Lumber and other resources are constantly in short supply. We should demand reparations be paid."

"You are thinking too small," the Sarmeer of Asha added. "The Realms need a new guardian, and with Emperor Zagu's untimely demise, Lord Baldric is in the perfect position to secure that spot."

"Do you think Legato Pierpont will just give up his power so easily?"

"His realm is in shambles. He is in no position to resist. Once Lord Baldric secures the guardianship, Adgul will have untold power and resources to command."

"That's not why we did this." Skorne propped his elbow on the stone table and rested his face in his hand, staring at his leaders through the gaps in his fingers.

"We can't let this opportunity pass us by."

"A new age for us has dawned. You must secure power."

Skorne sighed and closed his eyes. A hollow victory meant nothing. These people didn't care about the suffering caused or the pain inflicted. They cared only about the material.

"I will think through the possibilities before deciding our next action." Skorne dismissed the council and retired to his quarters, followed closely by Ekene, his retainer.

"Has anything actually changed?" Skorne turned and walked to the large windows on the far side of the room and rested his hand against Sera's rebuilt telescope which peered into the night sky.

His heart ached.

He envied Baldric and the time he spent with her. It was strange. How could he love someone so deeply that he never met? Only his past lives knew her.

"I don't know what you mean?" Ekene said, closing the ornate wooden doors behind them. "Everything has changed because of you."

"Am I not simply repeating what has been done? The same cycles of pain and hatred have eternally repeated." Skorne pressed his palm against his head. "A new age cannot dawn until the cycles have been broken."

"I don't understand."

"Sokaris scoured the universe, observing every world, every dimension—not one of them has created an age of harmony. I don't believe this can be done. At least not in the material form." Skorne pinched his brow. A thought clawed at his mind, but the words seemed foreign. He turned to his desk and grabbed a pen and parchment. Gripping the pen tight, his hand drifted over the paper, scribbling so the thought could escape the depths of spirit. "The Immortal Warrior was right about one thing. A forge shapes through fire. Perhaps only a cleansing fire will allow a new age to emerge."

"What are you saying?" Ekene eyes widened.

"A return to spirit. Ready your resolve to light the flames." Skorne gawked at his writing.

"You can't..." Ekene started, his voice trembling.

"You disagree?" Skorne cocked his head to the side as he studied the words scratched in ink. He raised his hand to his face. Why would it do that? The words it wrote were not his own.

"What... What is that? What's wrong?" Ekene stumbled backward.

Skorne grunted. "I'll need acolytes loyal to me, not Baldric." He held out his hand and drained the life force from Ekene, whose body crumbled to the ground. Skorne peered down at the words on the page.

"Stop. Please," was all he wrote.

Skorne scoffed and balled up the parchment. "Yes, a cleansing fire will do quite nice." He turned and peered through the large windows and out into the Kingdom of Adgul. "My work has just begun."

ALSO BY

Thank you for reading!

Please leave a review. Every honest review goes a long ways to help the author.

Check out these other works by the author.

Records of the Three Realms

The Songstress (Book 1)

The Bearer of the Seed (Book 2)

The Annals of Skorne (Standalone Novella)

Coming Soon

The Lady of Light (Book 3)

ABOUT THE AUTHOR

Joshua Killingsworth is a fantasy lover and author who has spent his life dreaming up worlds to explore. He enjoys stories of heroes set in worlds full of imagination and intrigue. When not writing, he can be found playing video games, spending time with his two kids, or hugging any and every animal he can catch.